MW01706235

LIGHTNING PEOPLE: DISCOVERED

Richard P West

I hope you enjoy my book

RPWest

Author and Publisher:

Richard P West
Box 543
NOTL, Ontario,
L0S 1J0, Canada

www.richardpwest.ca

Publisher's Note: This is a work of fiction. Names, characters, places, and incidents are a product of the author's imagination. Locales and public names are sometimes used for atmospheric purposes. Any resemblance to actual people, living or dead, or to businesses, companies, events, institutions, or locales is completely coincidental.

Printed in the United States of America.

Lightning People: Discovered, Book 1 / Richard P West -1st Edition.
ISBN: 978-1-7750602-1-5

Cover Design by Richard P West

Contents

1 Event

Sunday
18th October 1903

On the way to the village pub, Kenneth was shocked. The people he saw had coloured auras about them, hues of red, blue, yellow and green. The colours were mostly subtle although some were more intense. Kenneth hesitated to go further as he held his hands out in front of himself and stared at them. He could not see any aura about his own body while others around him radiated these beautiful shimmering shades.

Am I ill? I feel just fine even if I am seeing strange colours, he thought.

In the pub Kenneth continued to see auras around people. He felt at home in the King's Head. It had been his local spot for more than twenty years. Everyone knew him here. As usual, the pub bustled with conversation. There was the familiar smell of stale beer and hot food. His favourite roast beef dinner tasted the same as always, including the hot horseradish, which he adored and his wife, Helen, could not abide. Kenneth rubbed his hands against the leather arms of his chair to check if he could still feel textures, seeking some reassurance he had not suffered a stroke.

He was having his Sunday evening meal in the pub while his family was away for the weekend. It was his first meal since Friday lunchtime because he had spent most of Saturday and Sunday recuperating in bed.

Watching the patrons, he started to realise their emotions and state of health influenced the tone and intensity of their aura.

He knew most of these people and their histories. Now he could see a dimension about them, which could only be surmised before. Kenneth noticed their reflections in the mirror behind the bar showed no signs of an aura.

It was a strange experience watching people he knew through a new set of eyes, now capable of assessing people from a completely different viewpoint.

How long will this condition last? Perhaps it will pass soon?

Kenneth looked up from his meal to find 'Old Ben' standing next to his table. He noticed Ben's aura was pulsating and changing colours fairly rapidly. Old Ben seemed pent up to say something. Kenneth hoped he hadn't noticed anything unusual about his condition.

'Young Kenneth, it's not the same! He's not his mother's son!' Old Ben lamented.

'Who's that, Ben?' Kenneth asked.

'Who do you think? This new King Edward VII. He's not a patch on Queen Victoria!'

Kenneth noticed Ben's aura brighten as he spoke. He also noticed a strong shade of blue kept rippling over the predominant pale reds and bright greens.

'Give him a chance, Ben. It's only been two years since the Queen died. King Edward is new to the role!' he offered.

'Bah!' Old Ben made to walk away.

Kenneth jumped in quickly before he could leave the table.

'You all right, Ben? Feeling fine?'

Old Ben turned on him.

'Why did you ask that? I'm feeling myself!'

The invading blue shades of Old Ben's aura coincided with the tensing of his muscles and jaw. He looked in pain but it probably would not be evident unless the aura had given Kenneth the clue.

'You keep yourself to yourself, Young Kenneth,' he scolded and walked stiffly away.

I'll have to be careful not to pry into people's feelings in the future.

Kenneth suspected this strange new capacity was due to a recent accident he suffered on Friday evening.

*****

Friday
16th October 1903

Kenneth's job as a surveyor involved building roads, amongst other things. Solving the technical issues, which always crop up in construction projects, kept his mind focused. He loved his work because it provided many opportunities to inspect the world around him. Walking in the countryside and villages of Wiltshire gave him immense pleasure.

His home was Chippenham, a cross between a market town and a railway hub. Located in Northwest Wiltshire, it is close to Bath and Bristol with a direct connection to London by rail. It is small enough to be personable yet larger than a true village.

It was a beautiful winter's day. Clouds scudded across a blue sky. Rain threatened but hadn't yet materialised. As the afternoon advanced, the sky darkened. At this rate, it would be completely dark by 5:30 pm. Kenneth had decided to inspect a field where the Navvies would be starting work on Monday morning.

The field was on the side of a hill. At the bottom of the field, the ground was sodden and stank of generations of cow manure settling there. He skirted the wet area to locate where the road would enter the field on its far side. Sure enough, right where the mud is the deepest!

There will be a lot of swearing on Monday when we move those Navvies in here.

As he walked back to the gate in the hedge, he became aware of a strong odour, a bit like the smell of chlorine. Looking around, Kenneth noticed a dark cloud floating over the hedge. He realised the smell was not from chlorine, but was the scent of an impending lightning storm.

Then the heavens lit up as the ground shook. Kenneth was struck and then blacked out.

*****

Saturday
17th October 1903

Kenneth awoke in the early hours of Saturday morning with charred clothing, surrounded by scorched grass. After managing to stagger to his feet and wobble his way back to his bicycle, he rode home.

Being a man of a rather stoic, fatalistic nature, he understood he was alive and not seriously harmed. How that could be, he didn't care. All that mattered was he was not dead or terribly injured. What he did not want was a lot of fuss. Should his employer think he had been harmed by this incident, it might damage his future prospects of employment. Best if he quietly rested up and watched how things progressed.

He felt odd but not that unwell. Rather than being terribly burned, he seemed to be lightheaded and have a temperature. Fortunately, Kenneth's family was away, and so he was able to rest over the weekend.

To his surprise, any small burns and scrapes healed rapidly, and by Sunday evening he had felt well enough to go to the pub for a meal.

*****

Sunday
18th October 1903

The family arrived by the 9:15 pm train as planned. Kenneth was excited to see them but worried they might react to his changed situation. As they got down from the train, he could see they also had auras. His hope had been that his family would be unchanged. Their auras convinced Kenneth that he was the one altered by the lightning bolt.

Helen reached out to him. 'It's good to see you. Silly really—I've only been gone three days but I've missed you!'

Relief coursed through his veins. He had been worried his family would see some difference in him but apparently none was evident to them. His two girls hugged him and chatted about their visit to Bristol. They walked the half-mile to their cottage on the outskirts of Chippenham.

'How was your weekend, dear?' Helen asked.

'Very quiet, dear.' Kenneth replied honestly.

'Well, it's back to work and school tomorrow. We should get the girls to bed.'

With his family at home, Kenneth had to be careful not to blurt out observations he made based on their auras rather than their actions or words.

At work Kenneth quickly learned to use this new skill to help make decisions. The hues of his colleagues betrayed their weak positions or uncertainties. Being able to literally see how a person reacts proved very helpful when negotiating with colleagues or officials, or when interacting with the opposite sex. He found himself getting involved with women who showed interest in him. Knowing how they felt made it almost too easy to please them.

Using this new skill too enthusiastically led to awkward situations, and so he learned to allow it to guide him rather than relying on it too much.

*****

1903–1910

Learning to live with this enhanced sense proved to be hard work. Kenneth worked to avoid situations where he might show more insight than would be expected, in case they led to people asking too many questions.

He found it was much better to store up his perceptions and only use his skill when it mattered to him. Even then, he often refrained from using it at all. It was awkward to be given sideways glances from people who could not see how he had realised something they were keeping close to their chests.

It was particularly hard to reign in his skill when playing cards. The auras of the players clearly showed when they were pleased or concerned or bluffing.

When women revealed interest in him, it was very difficult to not let them realise he knew how they felt. They would give off bright yellow auras even when they were not obviously paying attention to him. The ease with which he could attract women brought a side of his character out that he had not realised existed. He found married women showed keen interest in him, and they also wanted to keep any dalliance most private. This led to a number of pleasant interludes.

Kenneth began to worry he had been altered morally as well as physically by the lightning strike. He knew Helen suspected his affairs. She was also showing concern about his apparently well-preserved condition. Although it pleased her, she could see other women staring.

'It's not surprising the ladies look at you twice,' she remarked. 'They can't believe how well you keep over the years.'

It didn't make him feel any better about giving in to temptations.

*****

1914–1919

Eleven years after Kenneth's incident, the war broke out in 1914. He realised his surveying skills were needed in the army. Deliberately applying to engineering and artillery regiments, he knew they would covet his technical skills. Also, he liked technical challenges.

Helen was not happy about him applying to join the army.

'You're too old anyway. So why would you try to enlist? You could be killed, or worse. You've hardly ever been outside Wiltshire, let alone going to France.'

'I won't be anywhere near any trenches. They need people with my skills to help lay narrow gauge railway lines behind the lines, or to do the mathematics to help lay the guns. So I'll be behind the real fighting. I might even be made an officer.'

‘Do you think so?’

‘Perhaps. We won't know unless I apply, will we?’

‘I suppose so. What will I say to the other women if you get accepted?’

‘Tell them the army needs my knowledge, and I'm younger than they think.’

His main worry was the doctor would fail him on medical grounds. Once he saw the doctor's aura, Kenneth could see he was just pleased to have a healthy applicant. Using his talent to see the recruiting sergeant’s aura helped him get through the vetting process. Lying about his age was easy.

When he arrived in France in 1915, he found his skill useful. Being able to see the motivations of his fellow officers and the soldiers allowed him to navigate the complex and hectic activities at the front. A perceptive colonel noticed his ability to read how people were reacting in the stressful environment and recommended him for a transfer to intelligence.

He immediately found a niche in this role, interviewing captured troops or fifth columnists. No one could hide from his vision—he knew when they were lying or not answering out of fear. Consequently, Kenneth had an enviable record of detecting spies, obtaining intelligence from captives, and finding those who were engaging in all sorts of criminal behaviour.

He remained in intelligence for the duration of the war.

*****

Thursday
24th July 1919

Upon returning to civilian life, Kenneth noticed people commented on how he never seemed to look a day older. Even his daughters, now grown and starting their own families, were pushing the point.

Kenneth had to go up to London for a business opportunity. He also made an appointment at a private clinic to have a full medical examination, but was careful not to reveal any of his personal particulars. The examination proceeded well and the doctor's summation ended with praise: 'You are in wonderful condition for a man of forty!'

Forty? Kenneth puzzled. *I've just had my fifty-sixth birthday*!

Before taking the train back to the West Country, he dallied on a footbridge in Paddington Railway Station. A number of trains with engines belching smoke and steam stood by the platforms waiting for passengers. He watched the milling crowds while pondering the implications of the doctor's conclusion. It was still fascinating to watch the mass of people, with their hues of red, blue, green, and yellow. When he had a chance to see hundreds of people all at once going about their business, he was in awe at the gift he had been given. Standing before a beautiful backdrop of colour, he smiled at how this had become normal.

Suddenly, Kenneth focused on one man. There, in the midst of the crowd, stood a man with no colour at all, looking just like people used to before his rendezvous with lightning! The man was staring straight back at Kenneth. Feelings of fear and confusion arose in him. Something normal had finally happened, punctuating the sea of unusual experiences he had lived with all those years. The man waved and started to walk against the flow of traffic, towards the stairs, which led up to the footbridge.

Run? What now? But Kenneth just stood his ground and waited for the stranger to approach.

He was a short man of about 30, and seemed to have pockmarks on his face from some skin problem. Without any hesitation, the man reached out his hand and greeted Kenneth in a voice with an unfamiliar accent. Possibly Welsh, but yet not Welsh.

‘My name is Creighton.’

‘I am Kenneth,’ he duly replied.

'When did it happen to you?' Creighton asked, as if they were talking about missing a train.

‘What happen?’ Kenneth replied, hoping to buy time to think.

‘The lightning strike,’ responded Creighton a little abruptly, as if speaking to a child rather than a man at least ten years his senior.

Chided by his openness, Kenneth responded, ‘Seventeen years ago. When did it happen to you?’

Creighton gazed out over the sea of commuters below, and then stared straight at Kenneth, before saying, ‘In the year of our Lord, 1472!’

2 An Education

Thursday
24th July 1919

Creighton took Kenneth by the forearm and suggested, ‘I think you need a strong drink. I could do with an ale myself.’

They adjourned to a pub.

Creighton took stock of his new companion. He seemed to be about 40 years old, five foot ten, with a stocky build, wavy brown hair and brown eyes. Kenneth had a glazed look in his eyes. His real situation was slowly sinking in.

Creighton ordered drinks, and then offered, ‘It’s a big shock when you meet someone else like you, who just walks out of the crowd. Please believe me, it’s a good thing you ran into me.’

‘I think it may help if you know a little about my story. I grew up in the Welsh Marches and got struck by lightning while working in a field. Everyone was surprised by my remarkable recovery, and so I settled into village life again while struggling with my new world vision. I made many mistakes, which made people think I might be bewitched. Frightened by this, I ran away and lived the life of a traveller.

‘In those days, there were many people who eked out a living driving cattle or sheep, running riverboats, or as inshore sailors. Eventually I learned to use my new skills effectively and started to be valued as a member of those societies. In my heart, I yearned to be settled. One day I stopped at a village, and with the little I had saved, I bought a small cottage and field. Then, I began looking for a wife.

'Mary and I were married and we did well with our smallholding. We were happy, except that no children came along. Time marched on, and of course, I failed to age. Once people from the village started giving me odd looks, I realised I must move on.

'Abandoning Mary was one of the hardest things I have ever done. Before leaving, I signed over the farm to Mary and took only enough money to help me on my way. Fortunately, I took one other thing with me. Mary had grown up in a Manor House—she was possibly an illegitimate daughter of the Lord of the Manor—and she had been taught to read. She then taught me!'

'How could you just walk away?'

'Kenneth, you have no idea how small the society I lived in then. People were afraid of anything different. Should they get scared enough, they could do bad things. If I hadn't left, not only would I be in danger, Mary would have been as well.'

'I see. You had to leave to protect her,' Kenneth replied.

'For many years I would make trips back to the village in disguise, looking in on Mary. She remarried and had a child. It was then that I realised it was me who had not produced an heir—not Mary!' Creighton continued.

Creighton thought Kenneth had so many questions welling up inside that it was difficult for him to focus, and so he stated the cruel truth.

'Kenneth, you have to come face-to-face with your new reality! You are almost immortal. You won't age at all, and so you cannot stay with your family as they age. You must leave them and start another life where you are not known. You must do this soon. Come back to London, exactly three months from now. Come to this pub and I will meet with you again. I will introduce you to the others, and we will help you.'

With that short speech Creighton got up and left, leaving Kenneth numb and frightened.

Creighton stood outside the pub looking down the busy street. A young lad, about twelve years old, walked up and stood beside him, looking up and down the street.

'Trouble, Boss?' he queried.

'No. You saw the man I went in here with?' Creighton asked.

The boy nodded.

'Follow him. He'll be taking a train from Paddington Station. Whistle up a few of the boys to help you keep a close eye on him for the next few weeks. I want to know everything he does, and what his family gets up to as well!'

'Yes, Boss.'

'Here's money for expenses.' Creighton gave the boy a handful of half crowns and a pound note.

'That's plenty, Boss!' the lad exclaimed.

'I don't want you getting noticed where he lives. So you'll need to have somewhere to hole up while the watching goes on.'

'Course', said the lad.

A younger boy trotted up and informed them, 'The lads are at the Station.'

Creighton nodded. *So the young fella had guessed something was up and sent for the other boys, in case they might be needed.*

'Thanks. Billy, you stay with me,' Creighton said to the youngest.

'The rest of you must watch this fella very carefully!' he said to the elder.

Creighton watched his young helper saunter off, and worried how they would cope in a small provincial town. They were used to the bustle of London, with all its chaos, noise, and smells. *Hopefully they won't stand out too much there and attract attention to themselves. Their Cockney accents won't help either.*

*****

July–October 1919

Eventually Kenneth got up and went to the railway station.

Kenneth found his train and enjoyed an uneventful journey home. He dreaded seeing his family knowing what he may have to do.

Creighton's lads kept a careful watch over Kenneth. Had he taken notice of them, he would have seen an aura about them, indicating a nervousness typically given off by people spying on others. The lads knew they had to regularly change watchers to avoid being tumbled.

The next three months were painful for Kenneth. Every time he looked at his family or co-workers, he would go cold with disbelief. Could he do what Creighton had done to Mary four centuries ago?

Every few days one of the boys took a train to London and reported to Creighton.

'Still nothing unusual, Boss.'

'You sure he only goes to work and spends his time with his family?' Creighton worried.

'Yes, Boss! Some of us think he is unhappy though.'

'Why?' Creighton asked.

'Well, when he is on his own and thinks no one is watching, he wrings his hands and runs his fingers through his hair. Feels unhappy and don't want his missus to know is my idea.'

'OK. You've been at this for six weeks now. Cut back on the watching. Keep a couple of the lads there just to monitor his activities, once or twice a day. Should he go anywhere, follow.'

With these instructions Creighton gave him another pound note for expenses and let the lad go on his way.

*****

Friday
24th October 1919

Three months after Creighton had met Kenneth, he sat sipping ale in the pub. He was not surprised when Kenneth walked in. Kenneth would immediately recognise him due to his lack of an aura. Kenneth walked over to the table and sat down.

They greeted each other and Kenneth accepted a mug of ale. Creighton could see Kenneth was nervous but clearly determined to see what might come of the proposed meeting.

Creighton calmly explained, 'We are about to leave on a complicated journey across London. Our route is designed so we cannot be followed.'

So it was. A series of taxis, buses, trains, walks in parks and down side alleys until they came upon a small square, somewhere close to central London. Without any hesitation Creighton took Kenneth up the steps of one of the row of houses. He opened the door using a key from his inner jacket pocket.

The house had been separated into flats. They took a door on the right-hand side and entered one of the small flats. It was tastefully decorated.

As Kenneth stood taking in the surroundings, Creighton moved a large rug and revealed a trapdoor in the floor. He opened the trapdoor and descended a ladder, gesturing for Kenneth to follow. The ladder took them down into a cramped passageway, which seemed to have been walled off from the rest of the cellar. Kenneth followed Creighton along the passage for what seemed like the width of four or five houses. Creighton ascended a ladder similar to the previous one. Again, they were in an apartment, not too dissimilar to the other. They exited the apartment, climbed a set of stairs and entered a large sitting room in an apartment on the next floor.

A number of people were seated around the room and on seats in the bay window. This house was at the corner of the square whereas the one they had entered was in the middle of the row. None of the eight people in the room had an aura. After some initial comments to the effect that they had not been followed, all eyes turned to Kenneth.

Most of the 'Lightning People' were men of various apparent ages, but only one seemed to be in his latter years. Two of them were female, one much younger than any other person in the room—apparently as young as 18.

Creighton could see from Kenneth's reactions that he had expected to meet a couple of people, not a small club made up of people with a similar sensitivity as himself. He had missed nearly all the introductions because he had been bemused.

Rescue came from the lovely young woman of about 35, who stepped in to act as spokesperson for the group. She was about five foot five, with a slender build, light brown hair, a fair complexion and grey-blue eyes.

‘Kenneth, don’t try to sort any of this out immediately. We have all been through this, at one time or another. It is always confusing.

‘Let’s go over the introductions again, more slowly. As you can see, we are all Lightning People. You know Creighton, and I am Elizabeth. Then we have Luise, Ivan, Frederick, Ralph and George.

‘We asked you to come amongst us because you need to learn what is involved for people like us. Although my body appears to be that of a 35-year-old woman, I am in fact 299 years old. About every 50 years, someone seems to be hit by the strange lightning, which creates people like us. In the past many of these people failed to work out how to use their skills to survive. Invariably, they were persecuted for being witches or warlocks. Most of them were killed.’

Creighton noticed Kenneth's surprise and injected, ‘Oh, we can be killed! We seem to survive disease, we recover from most injuries quickly, but we are not totally immortal. Being drowned in the witches’ chair or burned at the stake has been the fate of many of our kind. Accidents have taken more while murder, war, and bad luck have taken others. We are all, as we know it, from the Western European area. There must be others elsewhere but we are not in touch with them.’

Elizabeth continued, ‘When we find another of our kind, we seek to include them in our circle as soon as possible, before society at large discovers them. Creighton took a big risk approaching you in Paddington Station. You could have been turned by the authorities, and been used to seek us out. Or you could have been what we call a ‘rogue’, one who uses their skills to prey on normal people to rob or kill. If that were the case, Creighton would have been in grave danger.'

'Once you left the pub near Paddington, he had you followed. We monitored you for several weeks to check that you were as you had seemed to be."

"You were, and so welcome!" Creighton added.

She asked one further question, 'Kenneth, who knows you were hit by lightning?'

'As far I as know, no one,' he told her.

'That's good. Keep it that way,' Creighton advised.

Elizabeth continued, 'Kenneth, don't try to sort any of this out immediately. We have all been through this, at one time or another. It is always confusing.'

'Let's go over the introductions again, more slowly.'

'As you can see we are all Lightning People. You know Creighton and I am Elizabeth. Luise is the other female. Then we have Ivan, Frederick, Ralph and George.'

Each gave a brief idea of their background, mainly stating where they were from and when they were hit by lightning. The oldest was nearly sixteen hundred years old, while the youngest was one hundred and forty two years old. Kenneth was the first in their group for quite a while.

They then gently explained to him, he was overdue in moving on from his family. He needed to soon start a new episode in his life. No longer would he be able to share in his family's trials, joy or sadness. It was imperative that he distance himself by disappearing or staging his death.

Staging death had become more difficult than it used to be. Simply disappearing and starting over somewhere else had become the better option. Taking some money and movable valuables helps to build a picture of an individual who has run away.

'The idea of leaving home and family is appalling. Sadly, you have to realise there are really no alternatives. Getting through the first fifty years is the hard part,' Creighton stated.

A brief, but intense conversation ensued, about how creating identities and moving on was becoming much more difficult due to better I.D. requirements, and technologies like photography and possibly fingerprints. This only confirmed such steps were not going to be easy. It also showed the group saw in Kenneth an opportunity to understand these newer techniques and problems more clearly. Kenneth had grown up with these ideas, and did not have to rely on outsiders' advice, about them. The group thought Kenneth might be a valuable asset.

Kenneth knew nothing about how to disappear and start a new life.

Luise, the young girl in the group, stepped in. 'I suggest Kenneth and I should start another lifecycle together, as a father and daughter. This would confuse people who might seek him.'

Apparently, she had 'disappeared' into the London flat some months before and was keen to re-enter the world.

Some of the clan were cautious of the idea. Creighton shared their concerns. He also felt left out. Luise had been a favourite of his for many years now. There may be complications from having a new person in the clan.

Creighton knew he did not have a hold over Luise. She was a Lightning Person like himself, with lifetimes of experience.

Even though he understood Luise was far more than she appeared, he could not suppress the feelings of protectiveness he harboured for her. She would always be an 18-year-old to him no matter how long she lives.

Kenneth agreed to have dinner with Luise to discuss the possibilities.

Creighton reminded Kenneth, ‘It will be strange to speak with Luise. You will have to keep reminding yourself, this child has lived for almost two hundred years. She has more experience of life than anyone you’ve known before we met, just three months ago.’

3 Disappearance

Friday
24th October 1919

Luise and Kenneth made their way out into the world by retracing the path through the linked buildings. She easily found a bus, taking them out to the southeastern boroughs of London. They got off the bus near a pub in Dulwich and picked up a taxi, which took them to Lewisham. From there they boarded another bus, which crossed Blackheath. Near the entrance to Greenwich Park, they abandoned the bus and Luise led them through the park. Past the entrance to the Naval College and into a small laneway called Crane Street, they entered a pub called The Sailboat.

Luise not only knew how to lose a tail but also how to navigate London. She knew where she liked to go, where she felt safe. At the rear of the pub was an enclosed veranda, which hung over the River Thames. It had an interesting view over the busy river, which was crammed with ships, barges and tugs. Unfortunately, the Thames stank and its aroma leaked into the veranda, mingling with the smells of ale and tobacco.

Luise asked Kenneth to order an entree for each of them, with beer for himself and a Perrier for her.

Carefully, Luise checked to see if they could be overheard before talking about the future. Luise surprised Kenneth by telling her own story, thereby delaying considering the difficult steps to come.

'I come from France. In 1742 I was nearly 18. I was running an errand for my employer, the local Vidamesse, when I was hit by lightning. A peasant found me, and I was nursed back to health by the Vidamesse. Returning to work in the kitchens, I immediately found my new skill useful in avoiding trouble and pleasing my employer.'

'Did you not tell anybody about the auras?' he asked.

'No. It was so odd. I felt scared to tell anyone about it. First I ignored them. As I observed people, I slowly learned how to use the skill of reading auras.'

'What sort of place did you live in?' Kenneth questioned.

'It was a small chateaux surrounded by farms. Our community on the estate was not large, and it was very parochial. Being so young, I was soon noticed for not aging. My parents realised this first. Then the young men who may have asked for my hand, found me odd, and so avoided me. I started to notice the hues of the people around me were becoming more intense as they became increasingly unsure of me. In particular, the Vidamesse showed vivid green and pale blue hues while the Vidame glowed bright yellow. The most worrying person was the local priest whose aura started to change to a vivid red colour. He frightened me. If he had declared me a witch, I would have been burned at the stake.'

'I suppose a young girl would find it difficult to run away in those days?' Kenneth asked.

'I was too scared to even think about it. Then one night, they came for me. I was gagged and bound, then dragged away. They released me in a room in the chateau, one I had never seen before. The priest was there and glowed with so much red; I knew he was bent on killing me. My mistress shone bright green while the Vidame shone bright yellow. They both worked to calm the old priest, saying they would keep me there out of sight until either I aged a little or the priest decided I must die. I was terrified.

'For the next few days, imprisoned in the room, I was visited only by the Vidame and Vidamesse. I soon realised the Vidamese showed strong sympathies for my situation.. It was obvious the Vidame had strong feelings for me. Clearly, I needed to encourage these emotions, as it may help protect me.

'After a week or so, the priest visited again and insisted on seeing me alone. He shone bright red while he interrogated me.

'He raged, "How can such a beautiful child as you be in league with evil. You are so small and delicate, with your blue eyes and light brown hair. Yet you are not natural!"

'As he did so, I noticed his colouring would switch from bright red to flaming yellow in an instant. Before I knew quite why, I touched his face and found the yellow raging in front of my eyes. One more stroke of his old face and he lost control, taking me where we stood. To my surprise, I did not mind. My survival, meant that I had to keep this man from condemning me, and get the Vidame and Vidamesse, to shelter me. Whatever it took to achieve that, I had to do.'

'Both the Vidame and Vidamesse fell to my charms, and I lived for many years in that room. Early on, it was so boring that my health suffered. Death seemed a welcome friend. It was the Vidamesse who realised if I was to keep my health, I needed to be employed. My master and his wife taught me to read and do the books for the estate. I wrote most of their letters, read to them, and generally improved my own education.

'When the Vidamesse was nearly 45, she became pregnant! This was not only to my surprise, but also to the old priest's and mostly the Vidame's. A baby boy was born. Then within a day, the Vidamesse died. The Vidame brought the baby to me, to be reared in my room. The boy would be removed to attend a wet nurse but spent most of his time with me, until he was about five years old. His father then removed him to be educated by a nanny and a tutor.

'During these years the old priest died. Unfortunately, he died while visiting me. The Vidame had to remove the body, dress it and pretend he had been drinking with the old man.'

'Is that when they freed you?' Kenneth asked.

'No. For many years after, I resumed my confinement with only the company of my aging master to stop me from becoming depressed. The Vidame took to getting me out of the chateau in disguise, and travelling to Paris. There we would stay at different houses each time, and he would present me as his niece.

'In 1789 I was shocked when my master entered my chamber with his son, Maurice. I wondered if he had finally decided to expose me and hand me to over the authorities. He spoke to his son of many things beyond my understanding. They seemed to involve upheaval and danger.

'Clearly the Vidame was aging rapidly, and his son had grown into a young man of about thirty. He was a plain fellow with a limited intellect though it hadn't escaped my notice when he glowed bright yellow upon seeing me.

'The Vidame spoke to his son, "I entrust to you my most valuable possession—Luise! She will never age, and she will be totally faithful to you. You will have to keep her a secret as long as you live, or the people will burn you both as witches. Promise you will do this for me."

'"I promise," muttered his son.

'Before I knew what was happening, I was bundled into a carriage, loaded down with many trunks and boxes. Two other carriages followed us away from the Chateau, each driven by a trusted staff member. After many hours' travel over rugged roads and tracks, Maurice spoke, “Luise, we will take a ship to England so we can escape the Revolution happening in Paris. My father is dying and cannot make this trip. He has sent us to England with as much of the family wealth as can be carried. There we will have to start a new life. I will say you are my younger sister.”

‘For the next forty years, Maurice rented modest country houses in England. He took to tending the gardens, a pastime he loved and was good at. I managed our money by finding investments, which would keep us provided for into the future. Maurice had to be chided away from his gardens to complete business deals and sign documents as I could not be seen doing such things. He took houses in London and hosted dinner parties. I would study the guests for those whose colour showed the most promise for cooperation and the right business connections. To my surprise we were remarkably successful.’

‘Was your situation noticed by others?’ Kenneth questioned.

‘No. We still moved on about every four to five years, before too much interest in our private affairs developed. Maurice continued to age, and spent more and more of his time in his gardens. Eventually, I was presented as his daughter.

‘Then one day Maurice called me downstairs. The front door had been opened a little earlier, so I was particularly careful about being seen. I entered his study via a back door, across which hung a heavy drape, so I could peek into the room without entering it. Maurice stood pointing a pistol at a short man, standing opposite him. I realised immediately, the man had no aura. Whatever he had said, to Maurice, had been seen as a threat.

‘I walked into the room and announced, “I am Luise.”

‘The man replied, ‘I am Creighton.’

"Kenneth, I'll leave you the task of imagining the rest of my tale. I did, however, look after Maurice, until he died.'

Luise then let Kenneth have time to consider her story, before speaking again.

'You have to move on regularly. If you are young like me, the moves are more frequent, or you have to live more like a prisoner. Being older, you may have longer periods between moves but you will still have to disappear every decade or two.'

'Is this any way to live?" he asked,

'No, it's not! But we need to survive first, then live as best as we can between moves. Survival is our basic need. A good life comes second. However, we do have good times in our lives,' she replied.

'We all follow our interests whenever we can. Creighton likes to read fiction—not the heavy stuff, more like adventure stories. He smokes cigars when he relaxes. When he gets a chance to get away for a few days, he likes to walk in the country and stay at farmhouses. Brings back his past, I assume.

'Ivan, who you met today, loves to go to the Opera and Classical Music Concerts. His reading materials are heavier in nature: the Greek myths and long boring novels. New inventions and discoveries also fascinate him, but it takes a long time before he is comfortable with the ideas involved.

'Elizabeth is somewhat of a homebody. She keeps a small house and tries to live a sensible daily existence when possible. But she does love the theatre and the new moving pictures.'

'What about you, Luise?' Kenneth queried.

'I also love the moving picture shows. I adore new clothes and meeting men. Dancing, parties, and wine suit me well. When possible, I like to spend time in warmer climates, like Italy or Spain.'
Luise thought, *Kenneth is uneasy with his situation, but he can't see any other alternative.*

'What are you proposing?' he queried.

Luise outlined her plan.

'We will leave England and travel to Europe. The clan has ties in Europe, which need rebuilding after the war. While there, you can learn how to disappear when you need to, and other things we know. For us, you can research the new identity measures, which are becoming more prevalent. They may limit our freedoms in the future. You will also get to know the clan is not without resources. We use these to assist us when difficulties arise. Meanwhile, we operate legitimate businesses and accumulate wealth, like any other family. The difference is we have a much longer time over which we look for returns on our investments.'

'Where in Europe?'

'We will head for Belgium. The cities of Antwerp and Brussels are where our group mainly operates from.'

'Why Belgium?'

'It's a neutral country, spared from much of the politics of Europe,' was her response.

'So exactly how do I disappear?'

'That is almost too easy. You go home. When you are certain no one will be at home, take some clothes, valuables, cheque books. Go to the bank and withdraw as much money as you think you can. Write a letter, simply saying "Sorry." Mail the letter and then we will head for a port and sail away. First, we will head to France using your passport, then to Italy using a new passport we will get for you. After some vacation time, we'll move on to Antwerp using another passport.'

'It just sounds too simple. For my family this will be a terrible blow, especially for Helen, my wife.'

'Then stay and before not too long, Helen will lose you anyway once the authorities discover you. I can assure you, the life you have known will not be the same. Never again will it be the same.'

'I have done nothing wrong!' he protested.

'That will not matter to them. You are different, and they will see a huge potential in finding out how you are different. How they can get power out of either controlling you or learning how to emulate your differences or skills. What do you think the government would do if they could use your skills for spying on other countries, or even their own people? Even now, one of our kind has been held for more than fifty years by the French Government! There are too many bad people who want to be powerful. Far too powerful! We have learned this the hard way. We do not want to risk this again!'

'They know about us?'

'Yes!'

Luise watched as Kenneth thought over what he had learned. He sipped the last of his drink and then asked, 'At the flat, I heard a term being used that I'm not sure I understand. What do you mean when you refer to a chirper?'

'Oh. It's slang we use to refer to non-Lightning People.'

'But why chirpers?' Kenneth puzzled.

‘Frederick started it. He is a bird watcher and he noticed how colourful birds are. They remind him of the colourful auras given off by people. Birds merrily chirp as they live their lives and so he labelled the non-Lightning People, chirpers. We all picked up on the idea because it easily labels them. It’s much easier than saying, a person with an aura.’ Luise explained.

She saw Kenneth make a small smile and start to get ready to leave. Luise realised he had made up his mind to disappear with her.

*****

Two weeks later, they boarded a boat train to Paris.

Kenneth cried the entire trip.

4 Another Life

Wednesday
3rd December 1919

Luise and Kenneth enjoyed a holiday in Italy before returning to Northern Europe. She had rented a house on the outskirts of Antwerp. Little damage had occurred in Antwerp during the war, and so it was a pleasant place to reside.

Being a major port, it has many trading companies with interesting business opportunities. In addition, it is the centre of the diamond cutting and trading business, which provides more business potential.

'You will enjoy this town,' she told Kenneth as they passed through one of the old gates into the city. Luise watched him as he gazed out the taxi window.

Creighton joined them and helped to arrange various business details, like access to a bank account, contacts to get transportation, and other contacts if they needed various 'things done'. He then left them to check out other business to do with the clan.

Luise let Kenneth settle in before addressing a key issue.

'You need to learn to speak French. Once you have mastered my beautiful language, other languages will have to be studied as well, including Flemish! We often have to move across borders, either for our safety or for business reasons. It is much safer if you can understand what people around you are saying. Also, you won't have to rely on locals to solve problems.'

She spoke French with him. He tried to frequent French speaking shops and businesses in the town. They took short trips to Brussels and other places, not too far from Antwerp. In the southern areas of Belgium, they saw considerable damage from the recent war.

'Luise, why does the clan seem almost paranoid about remaining hidden?'

'Kenneth, you have to understand our situation. We cannot lead normal lives. How do you think society would receive people like us—even today, when most are much more tolerant? Who would trust someone who can 'see' their motivations? People would recoil from us. And how do you think people would feel about us living so long? Many would resent us. Our belief is it would not take much to awaken the sort of persecutions we have known in the past. We have seen the persecutions of Protestants by Catholics, and vice versa. Christians and others against the Jews. Need I go on?'

'But surely you see we are governed by fairer laws now?' Kenneth countered.

'Perhaps. Our histories are very long and we find it difficult to fully accept the changes occurring around us. It takes a long time to adjust to new situations. At the root of our behaviour is the need to hide the very things that protect us—our ability to see auras and our longevity.'

Luise continued, 'We also have to try to protect ourselves from those rogue Lightning People who have been turned, who see us as a danger to their survival.'

'Thank you for explaining this, but I am still not completely understanding it all.' Kenneth replied.

Then Luise received a letter from Creighton.

'Kenneth, this is how the clan brings us all up to date with each other's news. Look here! This is an embedded code, which could warn of danger or the need to move on.' Luise said and then wryly added, 'No one's mail is immune to being opened and read.'

The letter also gave Kenneth a contact who was looking for assistance with his business. She could tell this opportunity raised his spirits. Until recently, he had never been used to being uncommitted.

The job involved assisting a local company with exporting/importing products. Antwerp's docks and canals were undamaged by the war, and so provided an outlet for businesses across southern Holland, Belgium, northern France and even Germany. Large and small trading vessels could reach Antwerp from the sea, where they exchanged cargoes before returning to the North Sea. Once at sea, they could travel to the UK, France, Holland, Germany, Denmark, Norway or even into the Baltic. The clan sometimes used these trading vessels as way of travelling between various places, thus avoiding using the major transportation hubs, like ferries or railway stations. This was one reason the clan had a number of investments in trading companies and small shipping companies.

As they settled into this quiet life in Antwerp, Luise gently cultivated social contacts. Kenneth followed up by inviting people to dine or attend the theatre, which kept him fairly busy. It did not take long before Luise had identified business opportunities. Kenneth would fall into the role of the junior partner; her experience outweighed his by several lifetimes.

One night after entertaining a representative of a dairy cooperative, Luise surprised Kenneth by coming to his room. He thought she had managed to find out something during the evening, and wished to tell him about it. She walked over and pulled him towards her. Luise passionately kissed him and commenced to make love. He drew back and expressed concern. She laughed and retorted, ‘It was high time we became lovers.’

Much of the useful information and leverage they obtained came from her pillow talk with targeted businessmen. Few elderly men can say no to a beautiful eighteen-year-old, who seems to have fallen for their brand of wisdom and demeanour.

As an excuse, Kenneth expressed concern that Creighton would take exception to a relationship between them. She laughed and tried again to get his interest. When it was clear this would not work, Luise shrugged and said, ‘One day, and there will be many of those so I’ll wait.’

‘Creighton does have feelings for me, and yes, he does try to protect me. We don't get as much time together as he would like because it is harder for a 30-year-old man and an 18-year-old woman to set up house together. The story that I am his sister soon wears thin. People can just about believe you are my father but that won't work for Creighton.’

‘He particularly worries about me, as I sometimes behave like an 18-year-old. Even though I have lived many adult lifetimes, I still enjoy life much like most young women. I like nice clothes, young men, or any man, going places and having fun. Creighton comes from a more sober time, and being a little older when he was struck, is more cautious. His fear is I will over do my indulgences and expose myself. I know I won't. So there is always an attraction between us, yet tension.’

After nearly a year in Antwerp, a letter arrived containing a warning. Others had found evidence one of their enemies, a rogue Lightning Person named Samuel, was again active and could possibly be in Europe. Luise took the warning most seriously. Immediately, she reorganised their activities so they were much less exposed to random observation. Social contacts were reduced and more closely vetted. Through Kenneth, she employed a number of young people, as 'runners'. These runners took messages, quietly checked out people, and kept an eye out for strangers or any unusual events near their apartment.

Kenneth's contribution to this was to keep a camera at an upstairs window. When people were apparently looking around the neighbourhood, he would snap a picture. As the number of pictures grew, he would scour them for repeat visitors. He found none.

After two months of this cloak and dagger behaviour, it was beginning to feel unnecessary. Then Creighton arrived late one night. He immediately confirmed that there was a serious danger, particularly threatening himself. An old enemy named Samuel had been seen in Holland. Kenneth was ignorant of this Samuel, and confessed that he did not know who he was. In disgust Kenneth dropped his photographs on the table and told them both, 'You had better look at these carefully to see if you recognise anybody.'

Luise and Creighton examined the pictures and after a few minutes, she handed one to Creighton, who immediately exclaimed, 'Ah! He has been past this house. The fact that he did not seem interested in it means nothing. He is too cunning to give away his plans or intentions.'

Immediately, Luise moved to pack their things and business papers. 'We move on before dawn,' she instructed.

They moved to Brussels and settled into an apartment. Creighton planned to stay with them for a while as he organised the new bolthole. Kenneth mentioned this was almost as strange as when he was shot, just after the end of the war. Luise and Creighton insisted they hear, what had happened. Puzzled, Kenneth recounted the unusual events of December 1918.

'I was stationed in Paris, attached to the intelligence section of General Birdwood's staff. We were starting to think about how to proceed in Europe after the war, and we were also busy organizing troop withdrawals back to the UK.

'One morning I accompanied the general to a conference at a downtown Paris hotel. After a long wait to get to the main entrance of the hotel, I got out of the car first to allow the general an easier exit. I was shot. The bullet passed through my right shoulder and embedded in the car door, just before the general got out.

'Apparently the bullet came from an American service rifle in the hotel opposite ours. The building was occupied by the American Army. An injured American soldier was found inside, and he told how an American journalist had hit him and knocked him out. The journalist disappeared and was not found again.

'No one could understand why this American wanted to assassinate General Birdwood, unless he had lost relatives at Gallipoli or something like that. It was all hushed up! As soon as I recovered, I got quietly discharged from the army. Then I went home. That's it.'

'Who decided the general was the target?' Creighton demanded.

'Why would anyone, especially an American, want to shoot me?'

'How long had you been outside the hotel waiting to get to the door?' queried Creighton.

'Possibly three or four minutes, while others in the line-up got clear.'

Luise then asked, 'Were you visible through an open car window all that time?'

'Well, yes,' Kenneth answered, guessing where this might be going.

'Did you ever see a picture of the American?' snapped Creighton.

'No.'

Luise whispered, 'What was his name?'

'I was told it was Bobby Samuels,' Kenneth whispered, starting to see things in a different light.

'What happened to him? Was he not chased or caught?'

'No. My colleagues told me he escaped completely. Apparently, he switched identities with an American Army doctor who was dying of Spanish Flu. He then made it back to the US on a troop ship before it was realised the switch had been made. He disappeared when he disembarked in New York.'

'So,' Creighton mused, 'he knows what you look like, and possibly your real name. He hasn't been snooping around the low countries by accident. He may intend to finish the job.'

'But why? What is his motive to try to eliminate me?' Kenneth pleaded.

'My guess is he had a big move planned for that meeting in Paris, and you—a Lightning Person turning up out of the blue—ruined it. He wants vengeance,' Luise summarised.

'We have another problem,' she continued. 'He could find out where your family live and use them as leverage or bait. We need to get them to a safer place.'

5 Samuel

Tuesday
5th October 1920

Creighton immediately took control. He had dealt with Samuel before, and had a better pedigree on this topic than most. Also, he was well connected with elements of society, who for a price, could be enlisted to assist them in times of need.

Then Creighton took up his tale again to give Kenneth an idea why caution is needed when dealing with Samuel.

'After leaving Mary in the mid-1500s, I returned to my roaming lifestyle. Now I was more of an expert in using my skills, plus I could read and write. Literacy was invaluable in those days, particularly for businesses on the fringes of legality, where such skills were rare.

'The need to move regularly had not changed but it was less pressing when your associates didn't pry too deeply into your private life. This made me feel more settled.

'In the late 1600s, I was in London helping a group of people who acted as an outlet for smuggled goods. Knowing the sincerity of potential clients in business was crucial. The authorities were constantly attempting to locate the sources of such goods to eliminate them or extract heavy bribes. My skill in 'seeing' agents was of the utmost value to my associates, and so I became a trusted resource.'

'Was London a large city at that time?' Kenneth wondered.

'It probably had about half a million people then. For those days, it was a large city. It bustled with trade, both in the streets and all along the River Thames. Boats were continually arriving and leaving the wharfs that lined both sides of the river. Merchants had warehouses and other buildings behind the wharfs, where they either sold goods or transferred shipment to other places. Now the river is busy with steamers and the like, but then the boats were much smaller and there were many more of them. The best description for how it was at the time, is focused chaos. There were so many people trying to do their business, all in the limited space along the river. Then there was the complication of the tides in the river, adding to the confusion. You might have enjoyed seeing it, Kenneth.

'One day, I was visiting one of these places of business. My aim was to cement new business activities, which would remain in place after my next disappearance. I expected to disappear soon. It was my goal to put in place a system of correspondence, which would allow me to provide services to clients without openly visiting their establishments. Luckily, the principal of this particular business had taken me aside to conduct our conversation in private when a small group entered the warehouse. They were there to view merchandise—they were only shown the legitimate stuff! Naturally, I took a look over the group to 'see' if any potentially worrying persons were in the party. Fortunately, we were standing in the shadows at the rear of the premises. Two things immediately jumped out at me.

'The most surprising part was the presence of a Lightning Person in the group! The shock of seeing him almost made me blurt out an exclamation. He was a handsome, slim young man of about 25, with almost blond hair and blue eyes. He was a little taller than average and had a look of supreme confidence about him.

'There were also two others in the party, who showed flickering hues of green and blue. Their hues made me fairly certain they were paid agents of some kind, rather than genuine buyers. I whispered to my friend the danger from these agents. I also requested that the young blond man be followed from a discreet distance. It was important to know where he went!'

Kenneth interjected, 'What do you do when you see an aura of a person who is clearly evil or has evil intentions? Should we shrug our shoulders and walk away? Expose him by warning people. What?'

'Usually, if such a thing does occur, it's not easy to change the situation just by speaking out and so it is difficult for us to do anything. Should this occur, we definitely avoid the person from then on.' Creighton answered before going on with his story.

'I left the premises via a boat from the warehouse quay. The boat rowed down river to Greenwich, where I sought out another friend. I employed some of his resources to locate the blond-haired man. Carefully, I warned them to stay well away from him and to regularly swap the boys they used for such surveillance. I was only too aware how easily a Lightning Person could spot a tail, just by observing the distinctive aura such a person inevitably presents.

'Over the next few months, I expended considerable resources establishing who the blond person was and what the scope of his activities appeared to be. Amongst other things, I established his name was Samuel. A group of merchants were working with Samuel to try to locate and eliminate smuggled goods, and if possible, the smugglers. They were not above using unsavoury elements to achieve their goals. Most of the information I received, I passed to my associates, thereby helping them. All information about Samuel, I kept to myself.

'The intelligence I received revealed that Samuel had an associate. He was an old man who Samuel visited once or twice a week. On one occasion I rented a room opposite where they met and caught a glimpse of this person. He was also a Lightning Person! The presence of two of our kind in London nearly made me give in to temptation and declare myself to Samuel. There was something different about Samuel that made me feel uncomfortable and extra cautious.

'Further information was obtained when a fortunate opportunity presented itself. One of the merchants needed a chambermaid. A business friend was able to offer a reliable young girl to fill the role.

'Soon, this young lady was able to relay the gossip going around the merchant's kitchen. The merchant was becoming concerned about the association with Samuel, because some of the other merchants had lost large sums to him or his friend at cards. In addition, there had been a number of robberies at merchants' houses, where money and jewelry had been taken. There appeared to be inside knowledge of where to look and what homes to target!

'Based on this information, not only was I motivated to move up my next disappearance, but my associates also developed a healthy caution about where they kept their goods. They were extra discerning about who they did business with. Only the most trusted clients were able to trade during these times. The net result was the price of brandy—and other sought after goods—rose significantly, much to the merchants' pleasure.

'Suddenly, the situation changed. Someone had informed the authorities that a smuggler and a burglar had premises in Whopping. Late one night, their building was raided and contraband was seized. In an attic, stolen coins and jewellery were found. Two individuals were detained: an old man and his daughter.

'The merchants ensured that justice was swift! Within the week the pair were taken to Tyburn and publicly hanged. Tyburn is about a mile from London, close to where Marble Arch is now located. It was used for execution since the eleventh century. Crowds gathered there in a holiday mood for these events.

'I witnessed the hanging himself, from a building overlooking Tyburn. This confirmed the old man was indeed the Lightning Person I had seen with Samuel. Also, I saw to my horror, Samuel watched the execution from a carriage, standing at the edge of the square, across from where I had rented a room. From my vantage point, I could clearly see Samuel's pleasure as the poor wretches went to their deaths. The horror transformed into fear when Samuel turned toward me and smiled, one full of knowledge and terrible cunning! Clearly, Samuel had known far more about my activities and movements than I had thought possible.

'Seizing the moment, I descended into the street. I boldly walked over to the carriage and unnecessarily introduced myself as Creighton. Samuel nodded and asked when I had been struck. When told, he sneered "another recent", as if this meant I belonged to some lesser race.

'Not that easily put down, I simply requested the date Samuel was struck. The reply was simple but evasive: "I remember the coming and going of Jesus". He then added, "Beware, young Creighton! I do not allow young fools to meddle in my affairs. You may keep your young hounds trailing me for another day, after which it shall be my game to play! Au Revoir."

'At that point, the carriage driver seemed to know to drive on. He aggressively pulled the protesting horses into mid-street and cantered off, scattering the populous as he went.

'I sought a horse and followed along the route taken by Samuel. I found the carriage abandoned in Deptford, close to wharves where numerous vessels were moored. Later that night, I witnessed a ship pull away at high tide, rowed out in the river by two longboats, into the ebbing tide. The current helped carry the assembly down river. Standing on the deck in clear sight beneath a lantern was Samuel.

'I made enquiries about the vessel, discovering it was carrying emigrants to the new colonies in the Americas. In fact, that ship was part of a fleet, which had left recently. A young man had chartered them, on behalf of Lord Sainsbury. I knew better than to accept Samuel had taken the voyage to the New World. I sent emissaries down river to check if he had managed to leave the vessel before it headed out across the ocean.

'To check on Samuel in America, I financed a young couple's emigration to the colonies so they might verify if he had indeed reached those parts. No evidence came that Samuel had left the vessel. Eventually a letter reached me. The young couple had heard of someone matching Samuel's description. Some months after the letter arrived, a dispatch was received by the young woman's family. It told them the couple had been hanged for theft. Stolen property had been discovered in their lodgings!

'I swore never again to underestimate Samuel!'

*****

Creighton and Luise spent some time evaluating their new situation in Brussels and putting as many security measures in place as they could. During these activities, the depth of their relationship started to become apparent. Luise clearly did not see herself as being committed to Creighton but a deeper bond definitely existed.

One memorable morning, Kenneth was surprised to see Luise in the hallway dressed as a domestic worker with a shawl over her head. With her was another lady dressed in a similar fashion—only it was Creighton in disguise!

Luise explained that their disguises were to confuse any spies Samuel may have posted around Brussels. It allowed them to cover most of their faces with the shawls, so their lack of colour would not be as obvious as only a small part of their faces were visible, to any 'Lightning' Person's prying eyes. This dressing-up session made Kenneth realise there were going to be far-reaching effects from Samuel's presence in Europe. Creighton also banned Kenneth from leaving the house until they were satisfied all was well.

That night, they returned and spent the evening enjoying a late supper together. Kenneth retired early rather than being the third leg on the stool. The next day, Luise informed Kenneth they would be leaving Brussels that evening. Ivan would join him in a couple of days. She then provided him with names and addresses of chirpers who would assist him if needed. She also provided some information about their backgrounds. It was an eclectic bunch: a doctor, an engineer, a taxi driver, a housewife, a couple of criminals, and a policeman! Apparently, they all had money problems and were only too pleased to be their eyes and ears for a fee.

After an early start, Creighton and Luise left the apartment using a taxi. They intended to travel into Holland using a local train service. From there, their plans were unknown to Kenneth.

Kenneth spent a fruitless couple of days doing small chores in the apartment.

6 Ivan's Visit

Monday
8th November 1920

The taxi pulled up outside the apartment building. Ivan knew the apartment he sought was on the ground floor. He smiled to himself as he pictured Kenneth's face when he arrived. Ivan had not seen Kenneth since he visited the house on Western Square in London. Speaking Flemish to the taxi driver in the high-pitched voice that went with this disguise was uncomfortable. Having paid the driver, Ivan unloaded his bags.

Kenneth was looking out for him but was clearly surprised by his disguise. He had not expected a taxi to arrive with a woman as the only passenger. When Kenneth opened the door, he faced a rather bent old lady dressed in black, wearing a hat with a veil. Ivan blurted out, 'Get the luggage,' as he hobbled into the hallway. Once inside he straightened up and discarded the hat, veil and topcoat. Kenneth grabbed the bags and returned to the hallway.

'Ivan!' is all he could say.

Ivan appears to be about 44 years old, and when not stooped, of average height. He has black hair with grey streaks, dark brown eyes, and a slightly olive complexion on a slightly built frame.

'Please show me my room so that I can rid myself of this charade,' Ivan pleaded.

After changing, he joined Kenneth in the dining room where a cold meal had been laid out, plus beer, wine and a pot of coffee. Ivan smiled, shook Kenneth's hand and congratulated him in French. They both set to and enjoyed a good meal—with wine for Ivan and beer for Kenneth—followed by coffee and cigars. While Kenneth cleared the table and washed up, Ivan took a nap.

Later, Ivan asked Kenneth, 'How are you getting used to your new life?'

'Since we have become preoccupied with Samuel, most of the intrigue has faded. I still miss my family and am wondering what to do with myself.'

Ivan reassured him, 'Your feelings are normal. In fact, we all think you have adjusted well to your new situation. As for Samuel, I am under no illusions as to how dangerous he could be to us all! Kenneth, you are a new experience for us in the clan. Perhaps you do not realise it but we are a relatively new group. It has drawn together those you now know over the last 150 years. All of us met with the other clan members long after we were struck. We had already learned how to arrange our lives for both survival and our pleasure. While you are only just starting to understand what is in store for you, time marches on.

'You are also like me—someone who has enjoyed a normal life with a wife and children before being changed. In the clan there are just two others like us. Most Lightning People are younger. Those initial experiences we had prior to becoming what we are now, influence the way we deal with this life. Obviously as we gain more and more experience, we absorb new lessons and, in a sense, mature. All of this experience is built on the foundation of what we were.

'Being a slightly older Lightning Person also influences how we can manage our lives. Luise is the best example of the opposite, as she is not yet recognised in society as an adult. Her apparent youth restricts her choices in society and forces her to move on frequently. In fact, she was lucky her employer sheltered her. Her chances of survival would have been lower without their protection. Being older, we have far more leeway.'

‘Samuel is apparently fairly young, and yet he has survived a long time,’ Kenneth commented.

‘Perhaps his ability to survive speaks volumes about how cunning he is?’ Ivan suggested.

‘Have you ever met Samuel?’

‘No, but I have, over the centuries, seen the results of some of his schemes. My belief is, he is very old in ‘struck years.’ I’ve often thought about why he is so fixed against other Lightning People. Perhaps he was betrayed by one in his past? Or could it be he feels threatened because he cannot predict our actions from an aura? We may never know.

‘I must apologise for speaking in French. I feel more comfortable with French than English. My English is good, but I feel my Russian accent comes through more, when speaking English. It sounds unpleasant. Also, I enjoy speaking French!’

‘Where in Russia do you come from?’ Kenneth asked.

Ivan looked a trifle confused, and then tried to explain his early life.

‘Kenneth, you must understand that I was born in 346 AD. As far as I can tell, I came from a village somewhere between St. Petersburg (now they call it Leningrad!) and Moscow. It was probably near Novgorod. I can’t precisely say for sure.

‘Remember, then we were not Russians. In fact, I spoke an early form of a Slavic language. We were pagan people. We worshipped various gods and believed in evil spirits, dark creatures who lived in the forest. Most people were intolerant of anything unusual. Magic was considered to be evil, and abnormal people were considered to be suspect. Little chance existed for travel except by the drovers, traders and sometimes soldiers. There was little central authority, except for the local chieftain or warlord.

‘My father was a woodsman. He felled trees in the forest and we made charcoal. We sold charcoal to traders who passed through, or to nearby villages. I learned his trade and worked with him. My wife and I had three children before she died: two girls and a boy. Then I was struck by lightning and my son cared for me. By that time my father was weak and my daughters were married to men from local villages.’

‘Did your son question your recovery or see any difference in you?’ Kenneth interjected.

‘It was my father who realised there was something wrong with me. After I recovered, he asked me outright one day, what was different. I actually told him because I was so confused. He thought about this for a few days, and then told me not to ever tell another person, including my son. His concern was others would hear that I was strange. Perhaps one day, when they needed someone to persecute, they would come for me. They may even harm others in the family.

‘We continued to live as we had been. I found I could get a better bargain for our charcoal than previously. I became known as a person who got a good deal when trading for food and other goods. Soon, I was starting to be noticed. My father was aging rapidly. He took me aside to confide he felt he was dying. He told me to leave the charcoal living to my son, and leave forever.

‘I am sure he did not realise I would live for so long. He just thought my peculiarities were a danger to the family: “Join the traders of the roads, and become a warrior or a sailor. You must keep moving on.” So I left our house in the forest, and passed by the local villages until I found a traders’ camp. They were most cautious about letting me travel with them. Once I helped them with settling trades, their attitude quickly changed.

'I moved ever onwards for many years. I learned different languages, how to read, how to sail a ship. I learned about the value of goods, and of silver and gold. I know that I travelled through the Northern areas and reached Norway. In the east I passed through what is now Turkey, and at one time I went as far as India.'

Kenneth asked Ivan how he motivated himself. 'Is it enough to just survive?'

Ivan was frank, 'It is a struggle to not fall into melancholy. As I struggled to develop skills that helped me survive, I often sank into periods when I would drink excessively and seek out women to distract me. I would wonder why this happened to me. Was it just an accident or did someone do this to me? Was this one of God's—or perhaps Satan's—ways of taunting us? Then after probably 50 to 60 years of roving about, I met Tara. I was in Persia and shopping at a Bazaar. Tara walked up to me and asked my name. I was shocked because she had no aura, and so I shared my story. Her story went back much further than mine. She was then over a thousand years old!'

'Were you amazed when you heard she was so old?'

'It was a sobering moment. You have to realise she was the first Lightning Person I had met. Of course, finding another person like me was a big relief in many ways. For the first time since the accident, I had someone I could talk to about my situation. Initially it was a cautious dialogue, partly because I found it difficult to talk to a small, dark-skinned woman who appeared to be 25 years old. It was not in my background or a normal social convention to openly interact with a lady, especially when I was the junior partner in our conversations. Her brown eyes, almost black hair and sheer confidence made me feel attracted to her. It was her knowledge of our condition and how to survive in the world that was her true appeal.

'She taught me that our kind have always been part of the human race. It was only when people settled into stable towns and villages that we found more ways to survive. It became possible for us to travel between the settlements, hiding our longevity. We would take knowledge with us wherever we went, and so often became teachers, advisors, or traders. Life could be most precarious. She also warned me that some of our kind serve kings and warlords, trying to coerce others like us into servitude.

'Another danger she warned me about were the gangs of brigands. When they realise we have useful skills, they resort to kidnapping and threats in order to make us do their bidding.

'Tara taught me to understand we can prey on normal people because we have the advantage of seeing clues to their moods and intentions. "Makes it easy to cheat at cards!" was her mantra. Are we really good people or just another brand of exploiters?

'Once, Tara ran across Samuel and found him to be devious. We shared some years together and I learned much from her, including she had a strong streak of jealousy, which limited my scope of activities. In addition, it was hard for Tara to live a decent life in Europe due to her skin colour, limiting our travel options. I had stayed too long in the east and was afraid my white skin singled me out too easily. It was time for me to return to Europe.'

'She helped you understand our situation?' Kenneth asked.

'Her knowledge about building wealth through owning property, lending money, collecting jewels and other pursuits, was invaluable to me. We have two advantages. Firstly, in certain times property and jewels become cheap due to adverse events. Secondly, we have time to exploit this because our investments span several lifetimes. Our advantage is we can buy when things are cheaper and sell when the market is higher. This also applies to lending money over long periods. No one else wants to do that!

'I slowly learned to be a banker and investor. This is still my main role. With a group as big as ours, it keeps me occupied.'

'Is it enough to be occupied?' Kenneth pleaded. Ivan looked at him like a parent looks at a child.

'I have spent many years struggling with that question. Sometimes I have concluded we should be using our special skills to guide society. We have seen it all between us. But who are we to put ourselves above others? Not only that, often we get things wrong ourselves. So, the idea has problems.

'Then there is the whole meaning of life question. We get to experience more life than others, but we can't even answer the question about how we get the way we are! So how can we decide on the much bigger existential questions?

'Part of our time is spent trying to counteract the rogue Lightning People just to protect ourselves. This sometimes shows us the evil around us. It's difficult enough to deal with the rogues; we are not able to deal with evil in general.

'What we all find is, the instinct to survive is strong, even after hundreds of years! As experience builds, we have many means to help ourselves survive. Yet, it is a constant challenge. There are people looking for us all the time. Governments know we exist and actively seek us to study or control us like we're specimens. The bigger criminal gangs know of us, and dream of controlling us for their own ends. Rogues either want to destroy us (we are competition) or expose us. So Kenneth, your future will be full of pitfalls and hard realities.

Now and then one of us gives up and ends the cycle. We all feel this deeply, as we know how close we all are to that abyss.'

'Are you saying longevity turns life into drudgery?' Kenneth asked with concern.

'No. Life offers us so many opportunities for different experiences. Not only do we have the chance to travel to different countries and meet so many people, we also experience significant changes in social norms. This can be demanding, and also fascinating.' Ivan continued.

'Over the last few hundred years, social and cultural changes have moved much faster, which gives us a constant challenge. The sudden profusion of machines has astounded those of us who have been around for a fair time. Alongside these changes has been the joy of seeing so many developments in the arts. Can you imagine how I felt when I first heard Mozart or Beethoven? Or when the new painters started to change the world of art into the modern one we have today? For us these changes were exciting, and still are.'

'We have more trouble feeling comfortable with the political changes like democracy. To us it's a strange idea that people have the right to vote. For some of us, these are dramatic and seemingly dangerous changes.

'At least you won't be poor! My task is to teach you how to access funds should you need them. Be assured, we have not lived for centuries, for nothing.'

'What happens if I get caught by criminals or the authorities?' Kenneth worried.

'Don't worry. If we sense you have been lost, the source of the funds will dry up quickly! In return, you can teach me about this modern world and all the changes that are happening. It takes us a long time to adapt to new ways and ideas. In a sense we are like many old people, set in our ways. So having a younger person to tutor us in these fast-changing times is a good thing. There are so many things I hear about now, which I find it difficult to comprehend. Who is this Einstein anyway, and what is a fingerprint?'

7 Intruder

Monday
8th November 1920

'You do ask difficult questions,' Kenneth joked.

Ivan laughed, 'While you have many interesting answers and ideas.'

Kenneth jumped back into their conversation by emphasising, 'If possible, the clan should start to make sure they don't leave fingerprints when they go out, or even in their apartments.' He suggested that they should purchase thin gloves to wear whenever possible, to help avoid leaving prints for others to exploit.

'I must be getting really tired. I fail to see why it could be an issue for us?' Ivan queried.

'Perhaps not yet. As the authorities collect fingerprint records, eventually they will find two sets of these prints that match. If they were collected many decades apart, it will raise a red flag! I have also realised, if I can take a picture of Samuel, then the authorities or Samuel's people could take photographs of us. We need to avoid anywhere we could be easily photographed.

'Ivan, I foresee the police keeping records of fingerprints and photographs for posterity.'

Ivan considered this. 'I don't really understand how this might be done or how such records could be searched. But there is one thing I have learned over the centuries, and particularly in the last couple: things change! If you foresee such changes, then I should listen. It's agreed— I'll alert the clan. We'll see just how willing others are to follow your recommendations.'

Kenneth went to the kitchen to get some fresh milk for coffee. As he returned, he heard a noise and alerted Ivan. Together, they went to investigate if there might be an intruder in the house. Ivan was clearly prepared for unforeseen eventualities. He produced a small gun, which he held at the ready as they cautiously searched the hallway and the staircase. Kenneth stared at the firearm and Ivan sheepishly explained, 'You never know what dangers there are in this world.'

When Ivan opened the door to the small cupboard under the stairs, he discovered a young man. Ivan's gun made an immediate impression on the intruder. He shot his arms up in the air and declared, 'I won't cause any trouble!'

From the intruder's aura, Kenneth could see he was nervous and also confused. Kenneth deduced the young man had been listening to their conversation and heard what must have sounded like strange ideas. They took him into the dining room and tied him up prior to probing him with questions about what he was doing there and what he had heard.

There was no question they would call the police!

As he answered their questions, they could both discern whether he told the truth, lied or hedged. They could also tell how much he was afraid of them, as he responded to each of them in turn. After a short while, he showed little fear of Kenneth but retained a higher level of apprehension when confronted by Ivan.

It was quickly established that his name was Jacques and he came from Antwerp, although he was born in a village near Brussels.

Jacques explained, 'I was hired by a shady character to find out where the lady and you had gone,' as he nodded his head towards Kenneth to clarify who he meant. 'By luck, I knew one of the people who had helped you move, so I coaxed the address from him and came to investigate. I hid out, hoping to find out anything that might be valuable either to my employer or me. Then I took it upon myself to do a little breaking and entering and heard you talking. What I heard puzzled me.'

They both stared at him, studying his aura.

'Your gun frightens me. Please don't kill me to shut me up.'

Kenneth and Ivan thought he had heard too much for their safety and possibly his own.

'We should move,' Ivan immediately suggested.

Kenneth watched Jacques, fascinated by his aura, which was alternating between pale red and pale green. He wondered if Jacques was scheming, and why he did not seem more terrified.

Then Jacques spoke up. 'Can I work for you? No one knows I'm here. My only family is my mother, who is living with her sister because she is forgetful. Perhaps, if I worked for you, you could help my mother?'

Ivan made the circumstances clear to Jacque: 'We have no power apart from money to help your mother. You need to understand that you're in a dangerous situation. If we think you would talk about what you've heard, it would go badly for you, and your mother!'

Kenneth was shocked at Ivan's threat, but was surprised Jacques did not show too much fear. Some shades of brighter red but mostly brighter green flickered over the underlying pale green.

Jacques again asked if he could work for them. He explained more about his situation.

'I realise, should I work for you, there would be no going back. It would be for life!'

Ivan grilled him about who knew he was there, what he usually did for a living, his relations with who hired him to look for them, and many other issues. When it came to whether he was known to the police or criminal gangs, Jacques denied any connection. Both Kenneth and Ivan were surprised; Jacques' aura told them he was telling the truth!

Kenneth pulled out some photographs and asked Jacques to look through them.

'Do you recognise any people in them?'

Jacques studied them, and pointed to a lad who he thought had worked for a pickpocket gang in Antwerp. He had definitely failed to recognise Samuel!

Ivan asked Jacque if he could agree never to see his family again. Jacques responded that if the rewards were enough, he could do that. They could tell he was speaking the truth.

So Kenneth asked if there was anyone he would miss, or who might miss him. Jacques' aura showed that there was! He became embarrassed, and admitted that there was a young man he would wish to keep in touch with. The mixture of shame, embarrassment and love in his aura was evident.

Ivan asked Jacques, 'Could the young man be convinced to leave his present life, and start afresh, with no going back?'

Jacques' aura showed great surprise and delight. He told them, 'My friend, Thomas, is penniless and lives a precarious life with no friends and too many enemies. I have befriended him, but because of his situation, our friendship is kept secret. I am sure he can be persuaded to join me.'

Ivan waved the gun under Jacques' nose, 'Let me make it clear, Monsieur Jacque—you must NEVER tell your friend, or anyone, about what you overheard tonight.'

Jacques agreed, and they could see he was sincere.

Ivan went to his room, returning with a set of handcuffs. He cuffed Jacques to a stout railing at the top of the stairs. Then Ivan announced, ‘We all need to sleep and think about the situation. We can talk again in the morning.’

He waved his gun at Jacques, and pressed his finger to his lips to indicate he should make no noise or try to escape.

Kenneth took a long look at Jacques, who seemed content with the night’s outcome. He wished he could read Ivan's aura as he tried to believe he would not resort to violence. Perhaps his ability to read intentions from auras dulled his sense of understanding the normal cues. He would have a lot to think about overnight.

8 Move

Monday
8th November 1920

Elizabeth was staying in a safe house in Amsterdam when Luise and Creighton arrived from Brussels. She had not expected their arrival. Presumably, something had prompted their change of plans.

Creighton quickly explained the recent events.

'From what you have said, Samuel recognised Kenneth as a Lightning Person and attacked him out of frustration?' she queried.

'We are guessing that. So far, we've never heard of Samuel being so impulsive. That does not mean he cannot be. My feeling is Kenneth's arrival interfered with whatever it was he had planned. Samuel got angry and attempted to eliminate the cause of his anger.' Creighton proposed.

'What is of more immediate concern,' Luise added, 'is Samuel probably knows Kenneth's name. He could find out where he lived and possibly use his family as leverage on Kenneth. We came to see you to ask if you can arrange some way to keep Samuel from finding them?'

Elizabeth looked at them and said, 'I see. What are your plans?'

Luise answered, 'We plan to travel further into Europe to cement business issues that need attention and find some more safe houses for use by the clan. This will keep Creighton and me busy for a few weeks, and it will hopefully keep any prying eyes in London away from Creighton. He and Kenneth are the only clan members Samuel has seen.'

'We believe he has no knowledge of the rest of us. Let's hope we're correct. It could be dangerous to assume he doesn't have any knowledge of the clan. We really need some evidence of this before relying on the assumption.'

A worried Elizabeth added, 'I think I may have an idea how to get Kenneth's family into a safer location. It may take me sometime to achieve a good result, but I'll try.'

Elizabeth agreed to delay her travels into Scandinavia and Germany. She had planned to evaluate what the post-war situation was there and see how the clan's interests had faired. Poland and possibly Russia were also areas of concern for the clan, and she had planned to extend her activities into those regions once she felt that Germany was properly attended to. She nursed the thought, *I hope this delay won't make my future work in Germany more difficult*.

Elizabeth added, 'I will need to talk to Kenneth soon to ask him about what has been happening in Russia. I confess I have no concept as to what Bolsheviks are or what problems communism could create, for that matter.'

*****

Luise and Creighton left to explore the situation in other locations in Europe, once again in disguise. Creighton continued to grumble and complain about the need to adopt a disguise, even though he fully appreciated why keeping people off their trail was essential. When they changed trains at a major railway station, they would revert to more normal attire in hopes of creating a difficult trail for any possible followers.

Before leaving for England, Elizabeth also adopted a disguise, as a young gentleman, complete with bowler hat, suit, and spats. This would not hide her from Samuel's gaze but it would fool people hired to seek her out as a woman travelling alone. She attached herself to a small group of men when she got to the ferry and enjoyed the start of the trip, discussing the state of Europe after the war. All the men had been in the war and so Elizabeth gained some more insight into those years. She spoke to them in broken English and demonstrated her command of Dutch, allowing her to explain that she had spent the war stuck in Amsterdam. She had made sure she had a day cabin for the trip so she could limit the time exposed to others and allow her the chance to use a private bathroom.

Once back in London, Elizabeth briefed the remainder of the clan and then contacted some friends she had used in the past.

'Hello, Beth,' Elizabeth whispered to a lady of about 65, seated in a cubicle in a working-class pub near Charing Cross Station.

'Is Kate with you?'

Beth looked at Elizabeth and beamed.

'No, love. She's running errands down in Southwark. It's wonderful to see you again. Fancy me ending up being your friend all these years. When we first met I was, well you know,' then she whispered very quietly, 'just a girl.' She then held her hand over her mouth while smiling through it. 'Not supposed to say that, am I?'

'Not if anyone can hear you,' Elizabeth gently scolded.

'What brings you back to us, my love?'

'I need a job done and you girls would be perfect for it. I hope you can get away for a while.'

'Course, my love. Nothing but small jobs to help out body and soul round here.'

'Is Kate well?' Elizabeth enquired.

'All the better for being rid of that useless man of hers. Now that the kids have grown, she has a little bit of a life of her own. She is going to be so excited to see you!'

'Can I assume she is still trustworthy?' Elizabeth asked, even though from Beth's aura, she could ascertain both Beth and Kate would be entirely reliable.

'Course, my love,' Beth replied. She had not been offended by the question. She knew how important it was for Elizabeth. Beth was 12 when Elizabeth hired her as a kitchen maid. For some reason, Elizabeth got on well with Beth, and when Beth realised Elizabeth did not age, she became a long-term employee and friend.

Elizabeth broke all the rules by maintaining a relationship with Beth. She still has no idea Elizabeth can see auras, but she does recognise Elizabeth has good sense when judging people. When Beth's daughter Kate reached adulthood, they shared the secret with her. From then on, they lived separately from Elizabeth. When Elizabeth needs assistance with certain projects, she employs them and provides an annual stipend to ensure they stay committed to her.

'How are you in yourself, Beth?'

'Not bad for an old one. I need more rest periods than I used to but I'm not doing too badly. Course, you don't know anything about such cares. It must be odd for you to see your pals get old and die. Don't get me wrong—I'm not jealous. Kate and I feel privileged to know you and share your secret. That's special.'

'Beth, it's not all one-sided. I have to live a life with few friends and am constantly having to keep an eye on who is paying attention to me and decide if they are just being friendly or have more sinister agendas. Knowing you and Kate helps make my life more meaningful. You are the closest to family that I have, and I'm only too aware that one day, I will lose that privilege.'

'We're glad to help again. I'm sure there will be more times we can get together and we will be able to help you.'

'So Kate and you can join me for a few weeks?'

'Oh, yes.'

Elizabeth, Beth and Kate set off on a short vacation in the West Country. The ladies rented rooms in three houses at strategic points around Kenneth's family in Chippenham. They then kept their eyes open for people who might be watching the family. After a week, it appeared there was no surveillance going on. Elizabeth decided to move on with her plans.

Elizabeth got Kate to find a man to do some play-acting for them. He was paid to hang around the family home for a couple of days, in a conspicuous and somewhat threatening manner. It had been explained to him that the family owed money and the creditors wanted to 'send a message'. The man did this well and was most pleased with his reward. Elizabeth had made sure Kate instructed the man not to approach or talk to the family in any way! He was only there to let the family know they were being watched.

Then Beth went to the family's house on the Sunday evening. Once the door was opened to her, she asked to come inside quickly 'in case the man watching the house came back.'

When inside she whispered, 'I have had been sent by your husband. Your Kenneth has got himself tied up with entirely the wrong sort of people and is now on the run from them. He sent me here to get the family away so you can be safe.'

'I'm Helen.'

'Call me Beth. People who know your husband asked me to try to help you give his enemies the slip. I can do this if I have your cooperation.'

'How can you do this?'

'It's simple, really. You will move overnight and travel to another town. There, houses can be made available for your use. Your men will be offered work in local companies. We have done this before and are ready to help you this way.'

'I knew Kenneth was different but did not realise he was living a double life. I'd guessed he had been seeing various women during our marriage. He was a handsome man, in a rustic sort of way. He kept his youthful look when I started to age. I understood it was difficult for him if some women took a strong interest in him. Actually, I didn't mind very much. It was flattering in a way, that these women wanted my husband. He must have been up to other antics that I hadn't guessed. I'm sure these dark interests were what took him away from us. I realise now it was probably a good thing he left. Having his enemies taking an interest in us is not what I want though. So we will do whatever you suggest.'

'That's my girl,' Beth said.

By midnight the entire family had been drawn into the tale, and plans were outlined to move them to a safer place. It turned out that although Kenneth had left Helen and the children nearly all his assets, they had not really known what to do with them. The house had been sold and a larger house rented, where the extended family now lived.

The family was instructed to stay indoors the next day while the hired man kept up the pretence of stalking. Late that night the family was whisked away, furniture and all. Early the next morning, they made a visit to their bank and withdrew their funds.

Two days later, Kenneth's family moved to Falmouth in Cornwall. Three small cottages in the old town were occupied by the family, and the following day, each of the daughters' husbands started work at two businesses in town.

They were delighted with the move, their new accommodations, and for having been saved from the criminals Kenneth had managed to set upon them!

Elizabeth holidayed in Cornwall for a month while she kept an eye on Kenneth's family. Then she left Kate with that task for the next couple of months.

Elizabeth then travelled to Sweden.

9 George's Plan

Wednesday
24th November 1920

Kenneth wondered aloud, 'Can we trust Jacques for the long term?'

Ivan replied, 'Who knows? We can only try to create a workable relationship with him, and then keep a close eye on how he and his friend behave. Remember, they don't know we can see how they feel about things. Treachery is not too hard to spot. Should either of them show signs of wandering, we cut them off and disappear. They can't go to the police and so would be left to their own devices. If you manage it correctly and make sure they never know where you reside, it could work. We do have successful relationships with Chirpers, from time to time.'

'It's decided then. I'll work to make Jacques and his friend useful allies,' Kenneth concluded.

To provide a safety net, Ivan took on the task of arranging a secret bolthole to which Kenneth could escape in case Jacques proved to be a threat or was just not manageable. Although he considered it unlikely that Jacques could be turned, he wanted to be sure Kenneth would be safe. Ivan then left Kenneth and returned to London.

Kenneth put Jacques to work on house chores and arranged that his mother was sent a sum of money. He asked Jacques to write a note, which they sent to Thomas. The note asked Thomas to go to a particular place in Antwerp at midnight the following Sunday. Kenneth watched the meeting place for two hours before the midnight rendezvous. When Thomas arrived,

Kenneth pulled up in a motorcar and asked Thomas to get in, after handing him a note from Jacques.

During the journey back to Brussels, Kenneth talked to Thomas, asking about his life and how he met Jacques. Initially, Thomas was not open to answering his questions. Kenneth could tell from his aura, Thomas had not accepted he should trust Kenneth.

'You must be surprised that Jacques told me of you?' Kenneth asked.

'Yes.'

'Perhaps you should understand who I am and how Jacques came into my charge. Like you, I suffer discrimination in my life but for entirely different reasons. This causes me to live an unusual lifestyle. When I found Jacques had burgled my house, I could have punished him or called the police. After speaking with Jacques, I concluded he might be helpful to me as long as he is trustworthy. It was then I learned about you. My conclusion was if I brought both Jacques and you into my care, then as a team, they might be even more useful.'

Thomas' aura showed a softening. He clearly had not fully accepted the situation but was relaxing somewhat.

Less than two weeks had passed from the time Jacques was discovered when he and Thomas were settled in the house in Brussels. Kenneth spent many evenings talking to Jacques and Thomas, both separately and together. From these interviews, he managed to establish a good idea of their skills, their temperaments, honesty, gullibility and craftiness. He was also able to tell how much Jacques had told Thomas, which was very little.

Kenneth's understanding of his charges deepened as he interacted with them more. As he set them tasks or questioned them, he learned from their aura's reactions. Jacques and

Thomas were very different people. Jacques clearly idolised his friend. Thomas, although fond of Jacques, was mostly scared of the world at large and deeply committed to Jacques for being his protector and for his love of him.

Jacques was a willing worker and felt no resentment at being used by Kenneth, as long as he was properly rewarded. Thomas was very grateful to be in a sheltered place and would do almost anything (legal or illegal) if he thought he might remain protected.

Kenneth felt pretty pleased with his progress when George arrived. George was from Scotland and appeared to be about 50 years old. Kenneth knew he was the second youngest Lightning Person in the clan (after himself), at about 142 'struck years.'

He was a short fellow, who still retained his Scottish accent even when speaking French. He spoke in short, direct sentences and favoured a pessimistic worldview. Mostly the cup was half empty rather than half full. George had good organizational skills and had shown a talent for finding ways the clan could work effectively and profitably with chirpers. He set about establishing his view of how Jacques and Thomas should be employed.

George and Kenneth compared notes and decided how to employ these two men.
George told Kenneth that Ivan had decided this house should be sold and another was being set aside for Kenneth. George would arrange for another to be purchased for the new team to use.

He confided that he had dealt with couples like Jacques and Thomas before and had found them to be most reliable if treated with sensitivity. From his questioning George had established Thomas knew little, if anything, about the clan so he should be treated at arm's length from now on, using Jacques as the conduit. Most communication with Jacques would be by letter. They would have a house to reside in and a stipend to keep them from getting into situations that might be unpredictable. He outlined some 'improvements' they would encourage Jacques to work on.

From the new property, Thomas and Jacques would manage a small supply company for spices from the Far East. This would be done using the mail, thereby avoiding too much exposure to the public. George explained that this was a type of business the clan had been using for a long time.

They agreed they saw Jacques as the organiser, messenger, odd-job fellow, small-time investigator or researcher. Then George surprised Kenneth by saying that Thomas would be happy to just have a quiet life, but he harboured the ability to be ruthless if needed, even to the point of murder. Kenneth realised that the clan's abilities to read auras had matured beyond what he had so far achieved.

Now Kenneth realised that he had a long-term responsibility ahead of him as he groomed his new charges for their new life, and most importantly, made them a valuable asset for the clan. He had lots of time stretching out before him, so hopefully managing his two new companions would not be too distracting.

Once business had been dealt with, George and Kenneth exchanged histories. In Kenneth's case that was fairly simple, as George knew most of his story already. George did tell Kenneth about Elizabeth's plan with regards to his family.

Then he told how he had been hit by lightning.

'I was a trawler skipper in the North Sea, off the Scottish coast. The boy standing next to me had been killed by the lightning. Once I realised I could 'see' how people were feeling and reacting to me, I quickly put the skill to use. I love ladies and find the ability to pick out a woman who is interested in me simply by looking at her, too tempting! After a number of successes, I started to get heavy pushback from fathers, brothers, husbands and other suitors. This forced me to move to bigger towns and cities, so I could swim in a bigger pool and enjoy more anonymity.

'In London, I was found by the clan and inducted into their ways. They thought me a little reckless, especially when it concerned women. I also love a good party and can drink too much. Winning at cards is another vice of mine, which becomes easy if playing poker. But I have practical talents useful to the clan, like being a good manager and organiser.'

George then told Kenneth the clan was hoping he might help them deal with a problem involving a 'turned' Lightning Person. George explained, 'This is a lady called Dianna, who had been restrained by the French government sometime before 1850. We are unsure when but are pretty certain it was before then. Our sources tell us she appears to be about 40 years old, but we don't know when she was struck. So her real age is not known.'

Kenneth asked, 'What does she do for the French government? Furthermore, why me and what can I do about it?'

'I can only guess at how the French government has used Dianna. The clan discovered she existed in 1870 when Germany and France were at war. Paris was under siege. Frederick, one of the clan, travelled to Paris to put in place arrangements for various business interests, in case Paris were to be occupied. He found he was being followed. After losing one tail, he picked up another almost immediately. Flustered, he took an exit from central Paris but was still chased.

'Luckily, he got away by concealing himself in a straw basket on a wagon. From that refuge, he saw a female Lightning Person directing the search for him from a rooftop, looking out over the square where he had given the police the slip. She had no aura and so he realised she was a Lightning Person working for the French police. His lack of an aura made it simple for her to track him from the rooftops and direct the police towards him. He heard the police questioning people about where the 'spy' had gone. Fortunately, no one looked into the basket.'

'I think I met Frederick in London? But I can't remember much about him,' Kenneth prompted.

'He is our resident *Agent Provocateur*, as the French would say. When things get complicated, he's our best resource for thinking on his feet. Perhaps it's because he is Prussian? Odd really, seeing as he is such a family man. When not travelling on business, he keeps a home with a loving lady. Obviously, these arrangements have to be terminated every 15 to 20 years. He makes sure the ladies are well placed before he leaves them.'

'How long since he was struck?' Kenneth asked.

'Nearly 800 hundred years. Once Frederick told us of Dianna's existence, we sought out more information and over the years found out her name and apparent age. The date she was captured is really a guess. It is definitely before 1850. We haven't been able to find out where she lives, or more accurately, is imprisoned.

'Why you? Mainly because you have more knowledge of the modern world and its ways than we do. You grew up absorbing the new ways of this world while we're continually trying to catch up and adapt to its changing ways.

'As for what you can do, that's a really good question. We need to talk about it before deciding on a plan. Given your experience in Army intelligence, we thought you might have ideas on how to find missing people. More precisely, find people who are hiding.'

'Well, my experience was more along the lines of interviewing people. Having the ability to see an aura made the job fairly easy. I'll give this some thought.' Kenneth paused then. 'Does the clan think Samuel knows of Dianna?

George replied, 'Perhaps Samuel knows the French have a turned Lightning Person. Maybe in Paris, he thought you were him, and so he shot you. If that is what happened, then he must believe the person is a man.'

Kenneth thought for a while and then added, 'I think not, based on his extreme reaction when he saw me in Paris in 1918. He had not expected a Lightning Person to be there at all. So why do we want to get involved? Wouldn't it be best to let sleeping dogs lie?'

'She is a Lightning Person, and so we feel for her because we are the same as her. There is another motivation, one I tend to empathize with: Dianna is a woman. The clan is dominated by men, so it is gruelling to think of a female Lightning Person being imprisoned when she could add more variety to our small society.

'It's dangerous as we don't really know how far she has been turned by her captors. We hope she is a prisoner and wants to be free. There is only one way to find out. Will you take on the task of finding out more and seeing if there is a way forward?'

Kenneth considered the issue for a minute or so, and then replied, 'Well, it will give me a challenge. So yes.'

10 Germany

Thursday
2nd November 1922

It had been an unpleasant journey from Berlin to Stockholm. The weather had cooperated but the mood in Germany was disturbing. People had been impolite and were clearly angry at foreigners. Even Elizabeth's persona as a Swedish woman failed to solicit much pleasantness. Given the financial concerns the people were suffering in Germany, due to their runaway inflation, it was not surprising they were prickly towards her. Her concern was that it went deeper than that though. Underneath, they are angry at the world and blamed others for their woes.

She had expected to meet Ralph at the house when she arrived yesterday, but he had not yet arrived. Elizabeth wanted to compare notes concerning their recent forays into Germany. She especially wanted to discuss the recent bank robbery with Ralph.

While settling down to a light supper she listened to music on the radio. How she could sit and listen to Holtz in the apartment, was still a marvel to her. Even the music itself was a marvel. When she grew up, there was no such music in existence.

At 11:15 pm a taxi arrived and Ralph appeared. He entered the hallway, dumped his bags and immediately requested a drink. She poured him a cognac.

Ralph took a gulp of the amber liquid and exclaimed, 'I hope I don't have to visit there again for a long time. The people are desperate and very rude. Please let us speak Norwegian, so I may relax in my own language.'

Ralph is about 5'9", with a square frame, blond hair, and blue eyes. He is famous in the clan for being a good dancer, as he is very light on his feet.

Elizabeth went to the kitchen and put together some cold food. He thanked her and sat down to a late meal.

'What's this about a bank robbery?' he asked while eating.

'As you know, Kenneth sent us copies of the photograph of Samuel, including small ones for our chirper friends. The manager of the bullion trading back in Berlin had one, and he recognised Samuel when he visited the bank. He contacted me and I decided to warn him there may be possible problems ensuing from Samuel's visit to the bank. Before my message could be delivered, the bank was robbed by five armed men. One of the robbers was killed by the police, and two policemen were injured but the robbers escaped with some silver.'

'That will be valuable on the black market,' Ralph commented.

'Yes, but I was glad my note to the Bank Manager did not get delivered, as he would be wondering how I knew a robbery might occur. I certainly had not expected a robbery and I am glad no questions were raised.'

'Do you think Samuel knew we have investments in the bank?' Ralph asked.

'I'm not sure. I'd like to think it was just a coincidence that this particular bank that was robbed.'

'I guess one bank is as good as any other, as long as it has money or bullion in it.' Ralph offered.

'You know, I think you're right. How could Samuel know we're invested there? Even the manager doesn't know our true interest in the bank. It must have been a coincidence,' Elizabeth concluded. 'I feel a little better about it now.'

'But it still leaves us with a puzzle. Why would Samuel resort to bank robbery? It's not the sort of thing he has done in the past, as far as we know,' Ralph pondered.

'I don't know,' is all Elizabeth could offer.

With that, they both retired for a good night's sleep.

At breakfast the next day, Elizabeth expressed frustration. 'I feel the last year has been wasted. We spent a lot of time and resources setting up safe houses in Berlin and Frankfurt. Now inflation has ruined most of our business opportunities.'

Ralph countered, 'But thanks to the early warnings from Ivan and Frederick, we were able to convert a lot of our assets into fixed ones like real estate, bullion and jewels, or moveable ones like ships. That has considerably lessened the extent of the losses. You also never know—we may still have equity there, after the present madness has corrected itself.'

'That may be many years from now,' Elizabeth suggested.

'We have many years,' Ralph reminded her.

'At least we are comfortable here in Stockholm,' she replied.

Ralph went on, 'I know it's frustrating for the German-centred business activities, especially after the disruption of the war years. Add to that the chaos of our investments in Russia; it does look bleak. But we'll find a way through all of this, even if it takes 20 years.'

'I shouldn't complain,' Elizabeth responded. It is great to work from Scandinavia. Throughout the war years, we enjoyed it here. The winter sports are wonderful. Trips into the wild are good for the soul, and the summers have so many pleasant pastimes. We've been lucky.'

'I agree,' Ralph replied. 'Better than London fogs.'

They spent the rest of the day writing to the clan and business contacts, to try to stay in control of their essential interests.

That evening they decided to eat out. During dinner Elizabeth asked Ralph, 'We have worked this part of the clan's business together for almost 20 years and not once have you made a pass at me. Why?'

Ralph stared at her and said, 'I hope you are not offended?'

She laughed. 'Of course not! I'm aware how much you like women and wondered why you have chosen to be such a gentleman towards me?'

'You are my colleague and friend. I know you take such matters very seriously. I admire you for that and would not like to upset our mutual understanding.'

'Good', Elizabeth replied. 'We are a successful team and I respect you, as you also seem to respect me.'

'I'll drink to that,' Ralph responded.

After an excellent meal of salmon, they sat enjoying a glass of wine.

Elizabeth mused, 'Our decisions before the war, about how to weather the disruption, have proven to be wise in hindsight.'

'Concentrating the clan's business within the UK rather than Europe proved sensible. Even now I think it will be many years before we gain back full control of our rightful interests across northern and eastern Europe, and even France and Italy,' Ralph proposed.

'I agree,' Elizabeth replied. Then she changed the topic of conversation. 'What do you think of Kenneth's argument for using typewriters for our correspondence?'

'I have to admit in the long term it makes sense for us to limit our handwriting on documents, so we need to learn to type,' Ralph said.

'I don't want to learn to type,' she groaned.

'Neither do I but I think I will have to,' Ralph replied.

Elizabeth filled her wine glass and said, 'If I must, I shall. But I shall think of Kenneth for a long time, every time I type something.'

*****

A month later, the clan in London received a note from a contact they maintained in Southampton docks. The man worked as a porter, loading luggage for transatlantic liners. He believed he had seen Samuel boarding the RMS *Mauritania* bound for New York, in a first-class cabin. The clan's interests in America were limited because they had known for over two hundred years that Samuel had settled there. This made it difficult for them to follow up and find out where Samuel went or if he, in fact, took the voyage."

11 Search

Monday
12th February 1923

Kenneth looked at George with a slightly worried look on his face.

'What's wrong,' George asked.

'I'm concerned about moving to Bruges. It's a fairly small town, and it may be more difficult to stay hidden there.'

'Who says you stay hidden? You spent about seventeen years in Chippenham out in the community in full view of everybody. How many times did people walk up to you and say you were a strange sort of person? None, I'd bet. So why are you thinking you will hide in Bruges?'

'George, we have just been through all sorts of charades because Samuel has been seen and now you're saying to forget all those concerns. I'm not sure what you're thinking.'

'OK. Samuel has clearly moved on. He was obviously searching for either you or Creighton in Antwerp. Then he turns up in Germany just before a bank robbery. Now we learn he has gone to America on an ocean liner. What are the chances he will pop up in a little town like Bruges to look for you? Yes, we still have to be mindful of our security. We need to keep a low profile and watch our surroundings closely for anyone who may be spying on us or following us. But we still need to live our lives. The other reason I picked Bruges is because I'm pretty certain Jacques will never think of looking for you there, should he start to be too curious about you. Anyway, I like the place I've arranged for you.'

'Very well. Why do you like it?'

'It's called the Hotel Langestraat, and your room looks directly out over the main canal. From the hotel, it's only a five-minute walk to the centre of town and close by are restaurants, bake shops and most other things you will need. By the way, I hope you can swim?'

'Why?'

'Well, should you be discovered and you can't escape the hotel, you can just slip out of the window and swim across the canal!'

'Then what?'

'Well, there is an old tunnel opposite the hotel. It can only be seen if you really look for it. It must have been some sort of sewer hundreds of years ago. I took a good look. About 20 yards up the tunnel, it has been blocked. At that point, there is a grating which opens into an alleyway between the buildings. Get that far and you should be able to slip away.'

'Wet clothes and all, I suppose.'

'Yes!'

'I'll go there tomorrow and take a look. And thank you, George. Perhaps I will like it there.'

*****

Kenneth was using all his spare time to consider the problem of Dianna and how he might help the clan with regards to her. Apparently, she was the only known turned Lightning Person, although others may exist. They learned over time that some turned Lightning People had come to unfortunate ends.

After seeing the hotel in Bruges, Kenneth was pleased with George's choice.

'Thank you for your help, George. I'll be comfortable in Bruges. In fact, I like the hotel and the town a lot!'

'My pleasure, Kenneth.'

'Before you go, may I summarise my thoughts about the Dianna situation?'

'Go ahead. I'll pass on your thinking to the others.'

' I believe Samuel doesn't know Dianna exists. He probably thought a Lightning Person was helping the allies during the war. Then when he saw me, he assumed I was the Lightning Person, and that is why he shot me.'

'Why don't you think he knew about Dianna?'

'If he had known the French held a Lightning Person, it is most unlikely he would have taken the risk of being exposed in Paris. If Dianna had been known to him, I'm obviously not her.'

'Good point.'

'My other thought is, if the French did use Dianna at the Versailles Conference in 1919, then she would have to have been somehow introduced to the participants so she could assess their positions for the French government. Hopefully, at some of those functions, there were photographers and she was caught in some pictures.'

'Maybe she was but unless there is only one woman in any pictures taken at the conference, how do you know which woman to look for?' George asked.

'Hopefully, there is more than one of her,' is all Kenneth could offer. 'My plan is to search newspapers for any existing photographs and see what turns up.'

'Good luck!' George responded. 'What should the clan do if they identified Dianna?'

Kenneth replied, 'I think we should talk to Dianna before doing anything dramatic. If we try to free her, it might give the authorities, in France and elsewhere, ideas about the clan. We must hope they don't know how organised our group actually is, or that it exists at all.'

'So how could we get to speak with Dianna?'

'That is another issue entirely. Who knows?' Kenneth said.

Before he left for London, George inducted Kenneth into some of the clan's courier lore. The dos and don'ts of how to efficiently send sensitive documents, and where to send them.

A couple of weeks later, Kenneth heard the clan felt it was a good idea to complete the search for Dianna and try to figure out how to speak with her. Based on his assumptions, Kenneth decided to go to various libraries in Europe to look at as many newspapers as possible, from that period of 1919 through to the summer of 1920. He spent the next few months consolidating the arrangements in Belgium and putting the clan's business interests back into shape after the Samuel disruption. He then started visiting libraries in various cities including Paris, Brussels, London, Amsterdam and even Berlin.

Realizing he could not just rely on memory, Kenneth organised a person to visit bookshops to try to buy copies of old newspaper issues he identified as being of interest. In addition, he purchased a small camera which could be used with an electric flash. This could take a picture of a newspaper in good electric light, when using a long exposure. To help steady the camera, he also bought a small folding tripod.

Slowly, he identified and obtained back issues of newspapers and official publications from the conference. He was organizing a trip to New York to start looking into American newspapers, when he noticed a lady in a photograph he was sure he had seen before. He noted she had not been described as the same person in the two photographs.

Back in Paris he again visited the library and they gave him the use of a small room. The librarian insisted on inspecting the newspapers before he could leave, and he had to show his notebooks to keep up the ruse that he was writing a book about the conference. Once left alone, he risked setting up his camera and taking a picture of the page with the suspect image. If it was Dianna, the picture may not be useful because she was part of a group and not terribly clear.

Upon returning to Bruges, he received from London a copy of the other newspaper, in which he had identified the suspected Dianna. It was clearly the same woman.

Wednesday
9th May 1923

The clan had advised him of certain contacts who may be of use to him in Paris. Returning to Paris, Kenneth sought out a family whose ancestors had been assisted by the clan (specifically Luise) back in the 1850s. Kenneth knew the family was going to be surprised, when someone associated with their debt, incurred seventy years before, approached them. *After three or four generations, they may even feel the money is theirs by right?*

Kenneth took Jacques with him to Paris and used him to approach the family in question. Jacques came back and apologised, 'I did not go to the house you identified. I took one look and beat a retreat. It's a really prestigious location. The owner is obviously very wealthy and must move in high social circles. I felt I would be out of place and attract attention if I went too close.'

Clearly, Kenneth needed to check out the family himself by finding out who they were in society. They turned out to be merchant bankers and moved in the highest circles in Paris. Obviously, the clan's money had helped them become very successful. In fact, one of the sons sat in the National Assembly.

To be on the safe side, Kenneth put in place a fast and secure way out of Paris in case this family was too tightly entwined with the authorities. He then had Jacques watch the movements of the family patriarch until they had an idea of his routines. The next time he went to one of his favourite restaurants, Kenneth followed him in. The man enjoyed a meal with a number of associates. When he left Kenneth intercepted him before he reached the door. Kenneth could tell by his aura, he was not expecting any trouble and that he was surprised when Kenneth stepped forward.

Kenneth handed him his card as he introduced himself, using a fictitious name. The name on the card contained a secret code word, which referred to the loan between the clan and this family. Jacques was close by with a car in case things went wrong. The old gentleman eyed Kenneth to see if he might have met him before. He then eyed the card, and immediately his aura changed to bright green. Kenneth respectfully requested that he might have a few words with him.

Monsieur Picket turned to his associates and excused himself, explaining he had some minor business to deal with. He turned back into the restaurant and taking Kenneth by the arm, led him to a quiet booth towards the rear. A waiter followed them and Monsieur Picket requested coffee and cigars.

Kenneth had disguised himself for this encounter. He wore a beard and had deliberately dyed his hair and beard grey to try to age himself. Monsieur Pickett studied him for a few moments before speaking. 'My father told me this may happen one day. I had given it little credence and frankly had assumed it never would. This goes back more than 70 years!'

Kenneth saw his aura had turned pale green and was alternating to pale yellow. He knew he had his cooperation.

He immediately told Monsieur Pickett, 'This encounter is strictly confidential and should always remain that way. Also, I am not here to collect on the debt owed. My employers need a favour and a small percentage of the debt could be forgiven if the outcome is satisfactory.'

Monsieur Pickett, being all business, questioned, 'Should annual dividends still be paid in full?'

'Yes, until you are informed of any reduction my employers may grant,' Kenneth replied. Then he went straight ahead and told Monsieur Pickett that whatever happens, he should never let anyone see what he was about to show him. He passed two photographs across the table and asked him, 'How can I find out who this lady is, and if possible, where she lives?'

Monsieur Pickett used a small pair of spectacles to look at the photographs and to Kenneth's amazement told him, 'She is Countess Lamont. I met her during the 1919 conference and she lives in seclusion in a Chateau in Normandy. I have visited the Chateaux.' He then told Kenneth exactly where it was. From his aura, Kenneth could tell that Monsieur Pickett had had a relationship with Countess Lamont! She had probably been checking up on him for the authorities.

Kenneth cautioned Monsieur Pickett, 'You cannot contact this lady under any circumstances!'

Monsieur Pickett smiled and then responded, 'That is exactly what Countess Lamont's handlers told me!'

Kenneth turned the screws. 'Remember, Monsieur Pickett. Should you not keep our contact completely secret, we can and will call in the debt!'

To Kenneth's surprise, Monsieur Picket did not get angry, but insisted, 'I fully understand, and will never endanger our debt for any reason.'

His aura glowed pale red, showing Kenneth he really meant what he said. Kenneth took his unlit cigar and thanked Monsieur Pickett. He excused himself and requested he allow Kenneth time to leave before he set out for home. Kenneth took public transportation via a long roundabout route to his lodgings.

Jacques and the driver followed Monsieur Pickett for a few days to ensure nothing unusual occurred in his circle of friends, at the house or his place of business.

Knowing where Dianna lived was certainly a big step forward, but its location had been chosen well. It was in a provincial location, with just two small villages close by. Kenneth wrote to the clan:

It will be difficult to spy on the place without being noticed and even more difficult to try to contact Dianna. However, there is a rail link close by, which may be a way to get closer to her.

Realizing he could do little more, Kenneth returned to Belgium and had Jacques return to a quiet life as a spice retailer.

****

Kenneth bought maps of the area in Normandy. He also pondered why Dianna (Countess Lamont) chose to have a liaison with Monsieur Pickett? Much like Luise who would turn the heads of businessmen to glean information, clearly Dianna was up to the same game with Monsieur Pickett. To find out what? Not for her own gain, as she was held at the mercy and expense of the state. Most likely, her handlers had been interested in Monsieur Pickett and no doubt his business interests!

Kenneth realised he would need to use extreme caution moving forward. He set in motion the first careful steps towards finding a way to contact Dianna. Contacts were primed to locate someone who worked on the rail link, who was in need of funds and could be persuaded to report on any movements from this part of Normandy.

Also, he set out to find a client of Monsieur Pickett's business, who may have had dealings with his merchant bank over the last few years.

Lastly, he sought out a sleeper who could legitimately be seen retiring to the vicinity of the Countess' Chateaux—not a highborn person who would be expected to call on the Chateaux socially, but perhaps a doctor, or a lawyer, or a teacher who could rub shoulders with the keepers without raising too many questions. It needed to be someone who could also have daily contact with the local tradespeople, middle-class gentry and the local farmers.

Then Kenneth put the Dianna search into low gear until he could accumulate enough knowledge or other intelligence to formulate the next move in his plans. It was also a lesson for him because he realised this was likely exactly what Samuel had been doing for centuries. He may also have an intelligence network, buried deep in the social landscape.

Kenneth turned his attention to the developing technologies that might make life more complicated for the clan and himself.

12 Elizabeth

Tuesday
21st August 1923

Elizabeth heard a taxi arrive. She went to the window and saw Kenneth pay the taxi driver. Before he had time to ring the doorbell, she opened the door.

'So nice to have a visitor,' she said.

'Nice to visit,' was his reply.

'What brings you to Sweden?'

'I helped Ralph with a small matter in Denmark. After your help with my family's situation, I felt I should thank you in person. Also, I've never been to Stockholm before.'

'This is a nice city. The people are hardworking, earnest folk. My kind of people,' she replied.

Once Kenneth had settled in, found his room, unpacked and had a meal, they settled down in the living room with a glass of red wine.

Elizabeth gently scolded Kenneth, 'There was no need to make this journey just to thank me for helping your family to a safer location.'

'I know it's a little theatrical, but I am very grateful. All this cloak and dagger stuff with Samuel got me confused. Either I feel we are not doing enough to hide ourselves from him and others or I feel I'm getting too paranoid, just jumping at shadows. Your simple intervening with my family at least felt practical and not overly dramatic. It did me good to know it could be done, and they are none the wiser about any potential threats.'

'You should remember we did this not just for you. If Samuel achieved control of them, not only you would have been exposed to blackmail, we would have been forced to protect both you and them. Samuel would soon figure out it's not just you and Creighton he's dealing with. The longer he doesn't realise the clan's make-up, the better. As for what I did, 'let's just say it was a variation on a previous situation that turned out well.'

'Could you please tell me more about yourself?'

Elizabeth sipped her wine before speaking, 'I was struck in 1655 in Denmark, at the age of 35.'

Kenneth interrupted her, 'I still find it hard to believe that such a vibrant and attractive young women as you is really over 300 years old!'

'Thank you, but I am. When you have lived 300 years, you may see how amusing it is to have someone say that to you. Really, my age is still 35 even though my experience is spread across a much longer time.'

'I see.'

'I grew up on a small farm on Denmark's west coast. Our farm was close to a small fishing village. At seventeen, I married a farmers' son and we took over my grandparents' small farm, which was close by. We raised three children.'

'I tend to forget how hard it was for children to survive their first few months,' Kenneth muttered.

'It is always hard but was much worse then. My life was that of both a housewife and farm labourer, rolled into one. Ansgar, my husband, was an active lay preacher in the local Lutheran Church. He shared his passion for the Bible with me and we would jointly read it together in the evenings. In Denmark, we had been Lutheran for over 100 years by then. Being able to read a Danish Bible and participate in services entirely in Danish was very important to us. You could say we were radical in our religious beliefs.

‘One blustery morning while I was milking our cow, lightning struck. The cow died and I was burned a little, which kept me in bed for two days. While recovering, I quickly realised there had been a change in me. Ansgar was a perceptive man, and he soon realised I was not the same person anymore. One day he just said, “You always seem to know what I am thinking.” From then on he became protective. It’s as if he sensed that there was much more to the change than he could appreciate. He worried that in our small farming village, it would be noticed and I might be persecuted.

‘After ten years, we both realised I was not ageing and we would not be able to stay there much longer. We realised we could not take our children (then 21, 23 and 25) with us when we left. One day we packed up a few possessions and money we had been saving, made the farm over to our children, then travelled to Hamburg, in what is now Germany.’

‘How big was Hamburg in those days?’ he queried.

‘Compared to our small community, it was huge. Nowadays we would look at it like a small town. My guess is it was no more than 100,000 souls. Big enough for us to disappear into.’

‘Would you like another glass of wine before I carry on?’

‘Yes, please.’

With recharged glasses, they again got comfortable and Elizabeth continued her tale.

'Our lives in Germany involved moves to other cities or towns about every seven to eight years so that my lack of ageing did not create too much attention. Ansgar experienced a desperate internal struggle because his deep religious beliefs could not be aligned with his behaviour, protecting his abnormal wife.'

'One lovely sunny, quiet day, we had a surprise visitor. When there was a knock at the door, we assumed it was a neighbour. A visiting preacher had recognised Ansgar and found out where he lived. He called unannounced and immediately saw I had not aged at all in more than 30 years while he and Ansgar were both old men by then. He flew into a rage and called me unnatural. My husband worked hard to calm him down, but we knew he would betray us as soon as he could. Suddenly Ansgar grabbed our visitor and tied him up. We immediately fled the town, heading south into France.

'Once we reached France, Ansgar told me he was too old to keep up this life we were forced to lead. He insisted that we separate. He gave me all the money we had accumulated over the years. My plan had to be to get as far south as I could, using the money and then find somewhere to live that would allow me to hide my true nature. Ansgar planned to head back north to a monastic retreat in northern Germany. I eventually found my way to northern Italy, some months later.'

'Your husband must have loved you deeply,' Kenneth offered.

'He did. Some years later, I learned as Ansgar had travelled back through Germany, he was caught by our pursuers. He refused to tell what had happened to me, only saying, "she flew away and disappeared." His persecutors took this as an admission he had been harbouring a witch or a fairy. They burned him at the stake for heresy. I have never forgotten about him and how he must have loved me!'

'I'm sorry. I had no idea how close persecution came to your life.'

'It was a long time ago but is still very clear in my memory. Now I rejoice in the gift he gave me, a chance to live a full life. It is just a life so much longer than even he imagined it could be. Thank you for your concern.'

'How did you manage to survive further persecution?'

'Being a poor woman travelling on her own, I faced a precarious future. It was clear to me I needed to quickly find a male protector and develop ways to gain his trust. This kind of behaviour was well beyond my experience and moral outlook.

'I came across an older man and showed him I could be useful to him, both in providing comfort and in business matters. It happened, I chose well. He was a Venetian merchant who relied on numerous contacts to enhance his business interests. To his surprise, he found I had an astute judgement about the sincerity of the people he was dealing with, not knowing exactly how I managed this valuable trick. Being a practical man who both valued his business and his comforts, he made a bargain with me.'

'He undertook to discretely keep me in a modest but pleasant house, where he could visit me. I agreed to accompany him on visits to his business associates. In addition, he would pay me a small percentage on any business activities I managed to influence in his favour. I often dressed as a servant so I could witness his business meetings. In this way, I was able to direct him away from problems, or towards opportunities, based on my reading of the auras of his business partners. Simple signals often sufficed to guide him. Sometimes, a more direct intervention was needed so I could guide him more carefully.'

'The merchant became rich and I was well provided for, having little reason to spend the funds I earned. As he aged I sought out a new 'partner' from another town. Then I disappeared from Venice and took up residence with a man in Rome.'

'Did this become your strategy of survival?' he asked.

'Basically, yes. Through the remainder of the 1600s, the 1700s and into the 19th century, I continued this lifestyle in most of the countries of Europe. After the Battle of Waterloo, I decided to try living in Britain. This move proved to be a successful one because there were many merchants, and by now I was also very wealthy. The city of London was a perfect place to hide my money.'

'Clever.'

'One day in 1894 while living in Bristol, I noticed a 'non-aura' person passing along a street close to my home. Quickly thinking of an excuse to find out where this man was going, I instructed my servant to follow him and find out where he went. Luckily, she saw the man go into an Inn.

'Over the next few days, the man was observed by my servant, or her daughter, coming and going from the Inn. After nearly a week, I decided to act. My servant signalled the man had left the Inn, so I could step out of an alley into his path. Immediately when he saw me, he stood still.'

'I approached him and introduced myself. His reply worried me: "Are you turned?" Apparently, my puzzled expression showed him I was not a threat.'

'He then introduced himself, saying, "I am Ralph."'

'So you have not been with the clan very long?' Kenneth asked.

'Correct.'

13 Threats

Friday
26th October 1923

Jacques looked up as the shop door opened. He immediately knew something was about to happen. A small boy presented him with a note and Jacques rewarded him with a coin. Upon opening the envelope, he saw a neatly typed message instructing him to go to a location known only to a few by the name used. The message referred to the 'florist.' He knew this to be a code word for a small restaurant on the outskirts of town. After work, he told Thomas he had to go out but failed to say where. Thomas realised their benefactors must have contacted Jacques and so he did not press the point.

At the restaurant, Jacques sought entry to a small private room located in the rear of the building. The owner was expecting him, and so he passed through the main seating area and entered a door next to the kitchen entrance. The room was dimly lit and a figure sat in the shadows of a corner.

Jacques watched as Ivan studied him from across the intervening table. It was a little disconcerting how Ivan and Kenneth would stare at him when they hadn't seen him for a few weeks as if they had to remember who he was! Ivan was never one for extended courtesies, so Jacques was not surprised when he just told him to sit down, and added Kenneth would not be long.

Jacques was pleased to hear that Kenneth would join them. He felt more at ease with Kenneth than he did with Ivan. It was not that Kenneth was the boss or anything like that. In fact, he guessed Ivan had more clout in whatever organisation these men represented. Kenneth was just less menacing.

Some wine and soup was served. Ivan failed to occupy their time with any small talk. Once Kenneth arrived, and after a pause, while he studied him in turn, things proceeded more quickly.

Kenneth asked him, 'Thomas has a high school education, does he not?'

Jacques was surprised that the conversation concerned Thomas. Almost instinctively he became protective.

'Yes.'

'What do you think Thomas would say about having the opportunity to go to University?'

Jacques was astounded by the suggestion that his partner could go to a University. He had to admit that he believed Thomas would be thrilled by such as opportunity. Both Ivan and Kenneth seemed pleased with Jacques' positive response to their suggestion.

Jacques could not help himself but ask, 'Why would you want Thomas to go to college? What will he have to do for you?'

Kenneth smiled at Jacques' frankness. 'We do require Thomas to do something for us, and it will also be for you. We would want him to seek out information and opinions about the modern forms of personal identification, as well as modern forensic studies and communication techniques. By looking into these topics as part of formal study, Thomas will be able to develop ideas on where such things will head in the future. He will attract less attention as an enthusiastic student, compared to someone doing this outside of an academic institution.'

Jacques nodded his understanding.

Ivan broke in, ‘Good! That’s settled. We will advise you which university Thomas should approach and with whom to seek an audience. Be assured you and Thomas will be rewarded! So please discuss this with him and hopefully get his agreement. Remember, he is not to know who is behind this, and you will remain our exclusive conduit to him.’

Jacques knew this interview was over and he left. He knew his craft and so he returned, by a circuitous route, continually checking he was not followed.

Thomas was pleased but not surprised by this turn of events. He realised that their benefactors had a complex game of their own. He was not interested in what it was as long as it benefitted Jacques and himself.

‘Yes, I would love to attend a University!’ was his clear reply.

*****

Wednesday
14th November 1923

Kenneth had not visited the clan base in London for some time. He had been busy with his own tasks. Others were also busy. Some of the clan wished to discuss Kenneth's concerns about being exposed by modern technologies. They had asked him to meet with them in London.

London has a number of Victorian and Regency era squares. Typically, these are oblong with houses surrounding a private garden or park-like area in the middle space. Houses around such squares are normally attached, with three or four floors and steps up to the main entrance. Western Square is similar to the others. To the north of the square is the University College London, with its domed main buildings fronted by a large courtyard. Euston Road is north of the University, and it provides access to most of the major railway stations north of the River Thames.

Creighton, Elizabeth, Frederick and Luise greeted Kenneth. Ivan was also in London but had been called away on business the day before.

The first evening they enjoyed a party together. Frederick loved to cook and so they sat down to a wonderful meal. Luise enjoyed baking, which provided them with both dessert and treats for the evening. Clan members always kept adequate wines and spirits available wherever they resided. London was no exception!

The next morning Kenneth reviewed his concerns about technologies such as fingerprints and handwriting analysis as growing threats to their long-term security. Frederick and Luise did not like some of Kenneth's methods. Luise was against using a typewriter when sending messages while Frederick could not understand how a random photograph could be so dangerous. Creighton was not pleased that Kenneth was recommending less use of children as message runners. He had been doing that very successfully for hundreds of years and failed to see why it may be undesirable now. Others had expressed similar feelings.

By the end of the day, most of the concerns had been aired and a general acceptance of his methods was agreed. Late in the evening, Ivan returned. Ivan took a glass of wine and a large piece of Luise's bread pudding before he sat down by the fire. After enjoying a few mouthfuls of bread pudding and helping himself to a second glass of the Bordeaux, he addressed the company.

'I was called away by one of my people who operates in the city. Two days ago he noticed an odd advertisement in *The Times* newspaper. Certain wording in the advertisement caught his attention. He thought it curious enough to bring it to my attention.'

At this juncture, Ivan turned to Creighton and named his contact: 'Peebles!' Creighton nodded his understanding.

Ivan continued, 'Mr. Peebles operates a property management company in London. His father and grandfather ran the business before him. Prior to me taking over our interests in this business, Creighton was Mr. Peebles' contact. Others have dealt with the Peebles before our involvement. You see, the advertisement named Creighton and Kenneth!'

There were gasps from the group on hearing this revelation.

'The advertisement,' continued Ivan, 'had been placed by a reputable lawyer in the city on behalf of an unknown entity. In simple terms, it cited various unconnected references and named our two people. We all would have recognised the significance of the references but to a chirper, they would seem to be totally incomprehensible. Mr. Peebles certainly thought so, but he felt obliged to bring it to my attention because he was aware I knew Creighton! I assured him it made no sense to me and swore I had not seen Creighton for years. I then contacted one of my helpers and got her to find a number of copies of the newspaper.'

From his bag, he produced these copies. They took the newspapers, and the offending advertisement was read by them all.

For Creighton or Kenneth,
Have you been to any good hangings lately?
Paris is lovely at this time of year, but much better in the Fall!
Perhaps Antwerp is more to your liking?
Atlantic voyages are dangerous.
You can end up with much more than seasickness!

A letter awaits you at this lawyer's office.
Send someone trustworthy for it.
When asked who sent the letter, just say who it was, my namesake blessed.

There was a long silence until Creighton growled, 'It's a trap!'

Everyone agreed that it very likely was.

Ivan laughed, 'Perhaps? We won't know until we read the letter!'

He then put his hand into his bag and pulled out a sealed envelope and cried, 'Voila!'

Luise scolded Ivan for being too quick to act on the advertisement. 'We have never seen behaviour like this before. Who knows how much of a threat to us this letter could be?'

Ivan just smiled at her. 'I have not lived so long without learning how to spring a trap, and not get caught in it!'

Creighton queried Ivan, 'Are you sure we cannot be traced?'

'Certain!' Ivan responded.

Frederick was puzzled,'How did you know the answer to the question in the advertisement?'

Ivan stared at him for a few seconds and then answered, 'Samuel blessed David.'

It was agreed that Creighton and Kenneth would read Samuel's letter that night. The others would get their chance to read it in the morning.

Kenneth put down the letter after having read it three times. He shrugged and bade Creighton 'Good night,' as he left the living room to seek his assigned bedroom. Creighton had also read the document. Now he just stared into the coal fire's glow and thought.

Breakfast was a confused and somber affair. Elizabeth presided over the cooking while Creighton and Kenneth looked after the table. They served toast or bread as needed, kept the tea and coffee replenished, cleared place settings and kept on top of the washing up. The others took turns reading the letter between seatings at the breakfast table. Ivan just enjoyed a long leisurely breakfast and was the last to read the letter.

They decided not to discuss the letter or its significance until that evening. Each of them sought activities to fill the day before them. Some stayed in the group of apartments they owned on the square. Others went out to attend to some matter or other, or perhaps to just be in the world.

Dinner followed a similar pattern as breakfast, except that Frederick gave Elizabeth a hand in the kitchen. After their repast, they stoked the fire and pulled chairs around it. The letter was placed on a small table in front of the fire so it could be easily referred to if needed. They all smoked, including Elizabeth and Luise. Some had pipes, others cigars or cigarettes. No one wanted to broach the discussion just yet.

Creighton finally broke their silent smoking.

14 Insight

Thursday
15th November 1923

'Kenneth, you should summarise for us, what you think this letter means for the future. We all have more baggage from the past than you do, which will likely make us think less clearly about this letter. Also, you're from this modern world, which makes you the most knowledgeable about what may be going on out there, particularly where Samuel is now.'

Kenneth had hoped he could sit back and learn from the others. The nodding going on while Creighton spoke dispelled that notion.

Kenneth said, 'I'll read the letter first.

"Greetings young Creighton and even younger Kenneth,

I know you have 'found' each other but I wish to warn you against interfering in my business. You may think it is in America where my main concern resides, but you would be incorrect. Be careful as you make your living in Europe that you do not interfere with any concerns dear to me.

You know I have been successful far longer than you. My experience is an asset you cannot hope to equal. It might be safer for you if you join me. We might then enjoy a jolly time and live high on mutual success.

Perhaps this idea does not appeal. In that case, be forewarned that I can send some of my friends to visit you. They are not particular about polite behaviour and owe me many favours.

It really would be best if you saw sense and joined with my activities before you become troublesome.

Send your reply to the lawyer. He knows how to get it to me.

S

None of the clan had ever envisaged such a dramatic turn of events. They were used to getting strange looks, detecting people who showed distrustful auras, or frantic crowds calling for a witch's blood. They even faced uncovering government or criminal spies amongst associates, but not open boasting and threatening from another Lightning Person. They were clearly feeling exposed by this letter.

'Samuel has given a lot more away in this letter than he realises,' Kenneth continued. 'He is dangerously unaware of the threats to him in this rapidly changing world. My concern is he is too focused on damaging Creighton and me in some way, and not concerned enough about his own security.'

Frederick interrupted, 'We are concerned about *our* safety, not his!'

'I realise that is our first concern. My worry is he could be entrapped by his own arrogance. Either the government or a criminal organization will get hold of him. Creighton and I could then become targets for their interest. The good news is, he clearly does not know about the clan. This is an advantage we need to protect.'

'He directly targets you and Creighton,' added Luise. 'Threatening to send some of his tough criminal 'friends' here to teach you who is top dog. How on Earth he thinks you could be pushed into joining him, is beyond me.'

'Samuel sees himself as a natural survivor because he has managed it for such a long time. Unfortunately, his worldview no longer matches the reality around him. His total reliance on his own experience will be his downfall,' Kenneth said. He then continued with some suggestions for the clan to consider.

'I think we need to firstly organise ourselves so we are as prepared as possible to counter any threats from Samuel. Essentially, we need to ensure that the clan's activities are as invisible as we can make them around Creighton and myself. Should things go wrong and Samuel fulfils his desire to hurt us, he must not reach others. I also suggest I write back to Samuel.'

Gasps rose from a number of the company.

Creighton asked, 'Why do you think it's a good idea to write back?'

'We can use such a letter to reinforce Samuel's idea that you and I are the only Lightning People here. Perhaps we might try to link us in his mind to Dianna. If we are able to, we could plant some doubt in his mind as to our relations with her. Of course, we should not let him know any details, and leave him thinking Dianna is a man. I also would like to give Samuel the benefit of my views on the dangers he faces. My fear is he is much more dangerous to us if he is compromised than acting independently. It may well divert his attention away from us while he evaluates what I have to say. Should he see any sense in what I say, it will take him some time to readjust his ways, which might keep him off our backs for a while longer?'

Each of the clan members sat and considered what he had said. Occasionally they raised questions, which he answered as best he could.

Frederick finally spoke, 'This group cannot make a final decision. We here are mostly seeing the sense in your proposals. Perhaps you can write a summary of the information for the rest of the clan. We will need to get the entire clan together to see if this is how we should proceed. I think we may need to implement other procedures now we know that Samuels' gaze is clearly directed your way.'

Kenneth thanked everyone for their confidence in him. He then took the opportunity to push another of his ideas.

'We need to see how we can safely use telephones. In the future, we may need to take action quickly. The telephone could be an efficient tool for us. It will need to be carefully employed because telephone operators can easily listen in!'

There were various nods of agreement.

15 Paris

Tuesday
30th January 1924

Monsieur Pickett strode across the lobby of his family's merchant bank. It was Tuesday, his usual day to attend the board meeting. He liked these visits to the bank. It kept him in touch with business and the employees. Tuesdays had become the day he saw his two sons. They were so busy, he did not get to see them much outside of the bank. His eldest son, Paul, ran the business now. Claude spent most of his time on government matters, except on Tuesdays.

Since the visit from the strange man who had been interested in the Countess, he had been troubled. Up until now, he had not confided to his sons, the secrets behind their successful business. Paul knew enough of the outline of the story so he could properly manage the necessary business issues involved. Perhaps it was time to complete Paul's education?

On the way to the meeting, he called in at various departments to share some moments with employees. In one department the manager took him aside and quietly requested he come to his office after the meeting. He seemed nervous, and so Monsieur Pickett assured him he would come. Puzzled, he sought the stairs and walked up to the top floor where the Tuesday meetings were always held.

As agreed he called in at the manager's office after the board meeting. To his surprise, there were two other people in the room: a young man, who was clearly some sort of plain-clothes police official, and Countess Lamont! She seemed amused to see him, judging by her smile and the intense stare she greeted him with. Monsieur Pickett's manager was extremely nervous.

Courteous greetings were exchanged. Monsieur Pickett honestly said he was pleased to see the Countess again. The official's name was Leboudec. It seemed obvious this meeting had been set-up so they could speak to him. Monsieur Pickett asked the manager to leave them. He was clearly pleased to be released from any role in the proceedings.

Once they were alone, Leboudec wasted no time in coming to their business. He explained the meeting was two-fold. His purpose was to privately discuss with Monsieur Pickett the present unstable financial situation (especially in Germany), and how it might affect France through the banking sector. The Countess heard of his visit and thought it was an opportunity to renew his acquaintance. This seemed reasonable, except Monsieur Pickett was already aware of the tight reins the authorities were able to exercise over the Countess. No doubt, his recent encounter had somehow caused ripples in the corridors of power!

A discussion ensued about the serious economic problems in Europe. For about half an hour, Leboudec sought his opinions about commerce, finances and banking in general. The Countess only listened, leaving the content of the meeting to her minder. When the topic seemed to have been properly covered, the Countess rose and took Monsieur Pickett's arm, as she quietly asked, 'Would you do me the pleasure of showing me around your bank? I would like to see how such an institution works. Meeting your employees would be most interesting!'

So it was when an hour later they came across Paul in one of the offices. Monsieur Pickett introduced the Countess, and Paul offered her his welcome. It was clear to the older Pickett, his son did not approve of his father escorting this handsome younger woman through the office, on display to all the employees! The Countess seemed highly amused. All the time, Leboudec hovered about, keeping a close eye on his charge.

As they completed the tour of the top floor, the Countess spotted the elevator. She immediately walked herself and Monsieur Pickett over to it and asked if they could ride down to ground floor. Relieved they would avoid again parading through the entire four floors, he readily assented. Leboudec became perplexed when he saw the elevator could only accommodate two comfortably. He hesitated, clearly questioning if he should also squeeze in. He thought better of it. It would look entirely wrong to be squished into an elevator with a prominent banker and a Countess! As the door closed, he was seen hurriedly heading for the stairs.

As soon as the door closed, the Countess spoke quickly and clearly, 'Do not trust Paul!'

Shocked, Monsieur Pickett stared at her!

'You are being watched. A spy watches you at your favourite restaurant. Do not change your habits, as it will raise suspicions! Your visitor was noticed!'

'Do you have absolutely secure ways to communicate with your contacts?'

She apparently did not need an answer. A small piece of paper was produced from inside her bodice and she told him to put it down his trousers! Shocked once again, he complied.

She then launched into a loud set of compliments about the bank. The elevator arrived at the ground floor, where he could see more men, like Leboudec waiting for them. He graciously thanked her for her visit and greeted Leboudec as he reached the ground floor. The party then efficiently assembled and expressed their farewells before departing.

Monsieur Pickett had much to think about as he walked home. He realised that his son was sharing information with the authorities. If it had been Claude, he could have understood it. Paul was the eldest, and apparent heir of the bank. Something apart from money must be motivating him. Now he knew he could not pass on the family secret to him. *How reliable would Claude be?*

There were ways to reach benefactors in an emergency. These had not been used for generations. *Would they still work?* He realised he had to try.

On entering his house, he discovered it was in an uproar. Claude and his wife had arrived. They were distraught due to having to take their pet poodle to the vet. A car had run down the animal. Their distress was being played out in his house. Claude approached his father to ask if he could be with his wife tomorrow. Claude had to go to the legislature. Initially, Pickett was going to refuse. Upon reflection he realised being chaperone to his daughter-in-law would be good cover for the small errand he needed to run.

Pickett dropped off a small package at a lawyer's office the next day. Three days later the package was picked up from a lawyer's office in Calais. The following day it arrived at its destination in London.

*****

Monday
12th February 1924

Ivan read the tiny handwriting. It had been written with a tiny quill. He had not read such an ancient form of Slavic for many generations. The note had three parts.

Monsieur Pickett's account of the visit and a small piece of paper from the Countess which had two parts.

Its first part was the name of a trusted contact who could act as a go-between with
Dianna. She emphasised the need for extreme caution. The authorities suspect there is a Lightning Person on the loose in France.

In addition, she told of an old diplomat who crossed the Atlantic last year. He was surprised to see a man on the ship whom he had last seen nearly sixty years before. The man was slim and blond. When the diplomat had last seen him, it had been in France. The man had not aged a single day in the last sixty years.

Once the diplomat arrived in America, he reported the encounter to the security officer at the embassy. Now the French secret police have a description of a possible Lightning Person. She advised extreme caution.

Ivan wrote to Kenneth in code. He copied Pickett's and Dianna's notes, also adding his own thoughts:

Pickett and his bank were surveyed by Countess in the hope of flushing out a Lightning Person or an accomplice. Clearly, Dianna has ideas of her own. Perhaps she knew Monsieur Pickett had an odd aura. She may have even concluded during their previous encounter that he may be a contact to other Lightning People. It's clear she realises there is at least one other apart from Samuel because she actually saw Frederick during the Franco-Prussian War.

One thing we have learned from her message is that she is very old. The form of Slavic she used in her message is ancient. I could read it because I grew up using a similar language and learned variants of it as I travelled. If she knows this language, she probably learned it when young. Why she assumed other Lightning People can read it, is a puzzle to me. I assume she did not want her jailers to read it.

Good Luck in contacting the go-between! Be careful!

16 When it rains!

Sunday
28th December 1924

Thomas looked out the window and surveyed the scene. The sea was angry with white caps receding into the distance. Waves rolled up the long beach to break in cascades of white foam. During the winter months, the seafront properties took a steady beating from the Atlantic storms. It was almost New Year's Eve. He had arrived in Saint-Michel-Chef-Chef, Upper Brittany the day before to spend a few days' vacation while pursuing research for his university studies. This pleased him. A short break, from the overcast skies of Brussels, was welcome. Jacques could happily run the business by himself.

Having time to study in an invigorating new location will be a big help. He was new to the life of a scholar and had found it difficult over the first term. Not that he had failed—hard work had seen to that! He needed to absorb the student way of life and settle into some serious reading.

Jacques' suggestion that he take a few days away over the New Year was appropriate at this time. Thomas did not need to ask why he was here at this particular hotel. He also did not need any lectures about being careful. His life had involved a good deal of hardship and persecution, so he had developed a keen sense of preservation. Monitoring those around him was an important part of that skill.

Upon arrival, he immediately noticed the wife of the proprietor who had carefully appraised him. She seemed to pay particular attention to his hat. Or was it the new hatband Jacques had given him just before he left? *Remember to wear it*, he had said. Madame Dubois was a woman in her sixties, white-haired and well-dressed but not showy. She had impeccable manners and although curious, was not nosey. Thomas wondered if this was the person he expected to contact him.

The day proceeded well. After breakfast, he took a brisk walk along the seashore, enjoying the steady wind blowing spray in from the sea. He then used the sitting room as a study for the remainder of the day. Dinner was most enjoyable, as he found good company amongst the other guests. For Thomas, this was a particular treat. Too often people would be cold to him or ignore him. The guests didn't seem to care what his tastes were. They were all middle-aged and had all been there before. To his surprise, this small group of middle-class escapees did not flinch from him, as he had expected. He seemed to add a touch of excitement to their winter getaway from Paris. One gentleman confessed, he did this each year to get away from the family, after the responsibilities of the Christmas season.

Thomas kept his senses sharp as he evaluated his companions. Were any of them police in some form? He couldn't be entirely sure, even though his companions seemed innocent enough.

As the gathering was breaking up in the late evening, their hostess joined them and said a well-meant good night, to each in turn. She wished him good night, and most cleverly slipped a small packet into his jacket pocket!

Once Thomas reached his room, he examined the tightly packaged object. It resembled a sachet of herbs or blossoms, which people often kept in drawers to freshen their clothes. Indeed, it did have a pleasant smell. Rather than try to hide this 'gift,' he placed it in the drawer where he had put his clothes.

Thomas found the remainder of his vacation very much to his liking. Going home to Brussels via Paris, he used certain delays and short side trips to ensure he was not followed. Jacques relieved him of his 'gift,' and they returned to their pleasant lifestyle.

*****

Monday
12th January 1925

Ivan carefully opened the sachet, which had been forwarded to London from Brussels. He spread the contents on the desk blotter and found two tightly folded pieces of delicate paper. Considerable patience was needed to unfold each piece of paper without damaging it. Ivan marvelled at the tiny writing and the skill used to write only in areas not exposed once the paper had been folded. Dianna had clearly used this method many times before. Again, the same ancient version of the Slavic language had been employed. After two hours, he had translated both messages.

The first message had been written before the interaction with Monsieur Pickett while the second message included more recent information. From the older message, Ivan learned exactly how Dianna might be snatched away from her French minders. It would be risky and possibly dangerous, especially if she were fully turned. This needed careful research and consideration.

The second message provided some further information and details about her jailers' organization. She also indicated Samuel had been described in a French extradition warrant to the US government.

Ivan realised this might be dangerous for Samuel, should the US government follow up aggressively to comply with the French request. Even if the US government failed to catch Samuel, it would be difficult if his criminal associates found he had a price on his head!

For the first time, Ivan used a telephone to make clan arrangements. He called Kenneth and used their new code words to let him know there was a reason to meet. Ivan then settled down to a pleasant meal followed by a brandy and a cigar. As he was relaxing with a second brandy, the alarm bell connected to the downstairs flat they used as their entry point rang! Cautiously, he looked through the curtains into the street. Four young lads were crowding the bottom front steps of the flat along street. They seemed agitated.

Ivan was not comfortable! Creighton had spent a good deal of his time ensuring his lads did not know about this house. Fortunately, Ivan was occupying the corner house where most of the clan meetings were held. Frederick was in the flat by the other entrance to their accommodations.

*****

Thursday
22nd January 1925

Frederick had heard the doorbell ring in the ground floor flat. He'd opened a drawer and retrieved a pistol.

Before answering the door, he had pressed a button hidden next to the fireplace. This would raise the alarm for Ivan in the main house, and he knew he would monitor what was happening from the front bay window.

Very slowly he opened the front door and put on his best innocent act to disarm those on the front steps. On the top steps were three lads supporting, a comatose Creighton, with four more on the lower step! The eldest of the boys immediately started to apologise for coming to the house. He had not known what else to do.

Frederick ushered them all into the front room. He also carefully pressed the hidden button three times to signal to Ivan there was no immediate danger. Creighton had been laid on the sofa. It was clear he had been severely beaten. Frederick turned to the lad who had first spoken and asked what happened.

He shrugged and pointed at a small lad. 'About an hour ago, he came dashing into our den. He had been with 'the boss,' when some men approached him. He made himself scarce, then doubled back a few minutes after. The boss was laid out, just like this. We rushed over there and brought him here. I know I shouldn't have, as I am not supposed to know about this house. I didn't know what else to do!'

Frederick looked at the seven young faces and studied their auras. Each showed serious concern, anger and determination. They were not the auras of cunning, treachery or greed! He reached into his pocket and pulled out a number of half-crowns. Addressing the eldest, he instructed, 'Take these. Get a doctor and tell him to come here by taxicab. You ride up with the driver and take an indirect route!'
The lad nodded and was gone. Frederick then turned to the remaining six and handed over the last two half-crowns, 'You,

except for young Georgie, spread out and watch the roads around this place. Do not speak to anyone about what you know. Let me know if you see anyone watching here or acting suspiciously. You'll need food and drink, so run to a pie shop for it.'

As one, the five lads turned and were gone. They knew how to do this task. It was their trade.

He told Georgie to watch the boss while he went to the kitchen to boil some water. An hour later, the boss had been seen by a doctor and had his wounds cleaned and bandaged. Doctor Benson felt he should be sent to a hospital but Frederick refused. The doctor's concern was that Creighton may have had internal injuries or a skull fracture. The doctor was paid well for his visit. Dr. Benson knew nothing of Creighton's regenerative capabilities and so had no concept of how Creighton might recover. Frederick hoped he had judged it correctly and that Creighton would be able to overcome his injuries.

Once alone, he turned to Georgie and questioned him about the men who had attacked the boss. Georgie was positive these men were part of a gang located in the east end. He knew the gang had known the boss but did not understand why they would turn on him.

After dipping deep into his trouser pocket, he gave Georgie two shillings and a pound note for his assistance. Georgie's eyes opened wide when he was entrusted with such a large sum. He was beaming because two shillings was a lot of money for him.

'Take this pound and give it to your leader. Ask him to keep the boys on watch until I tell him otherwise. If he needs more money, he should send you here for it!'

Georgie took the money, tipped his cap at the boss and then at Frederick, turned and was gone.

Once the coast was clear, Frederick lifted the trap door in the floor. Ivan popped through, pistol in hand in case of trouble. He walked over to Creighton and swore.

Frederick filled Ivan in on the intelligence he had gleaned from the lads. Ivan nodded and started down the ladder below the trap door.

He spoke over his disappearing shoulder, 'I'll instigate the move to the other house.'

Frederick returned to nursing Creighton. Towards midnight, Creighton's condition worsened and his breathing was so shallow, Frederick had convinced himself he was dead. Using a mirror he managed to detect breathing, although he could not detect Creighton's pulse because it was so weak. Creighton's skin had turned a dreadful shade of grey, adding to the impression he had passed away. Frederick realised Creighton could die. If he did live, it would be useful if his enemies believed they had rid themselves of him!

Georgie was discreetly keeping an eye on the house from the small park in the square. Using a light in the window, Frederick signalled to the young boy that he was needed. Moments later a faint tap came at the door. Georgie came into the front room and viewed Creighton's body. Georgie cried!

He sent Georgie to get the lads, two or three at a time, to say their farewells to the boss. Then they returned to their duties, watching the roads around the house.

By the following evening, all traces of the clan's occupation of the houses on the square had gone. Letters had gone out to distant contacts, to the effect that these people should move into the flat, which had just been vacated. The trapdoor was sealed shut from below.

The lads who were patiently standing guard received a note, delivered by Georgie. Inside was a hundred pounds! Their instructions were to use the money to find decent employment and to abandon their lives on the street. All watch on the house should cease.

Meanwhile, Creighton had been spirited down to the basement and up into the main house. In the dead of night, he had been passed over the back wall into the garden of the house behind. Quietly, he had passed through the premises into a motorcar in the next street. From there he travelled until he entered a house in Bromley, about nine miles southeast of London.

*****

Saturday
24th January 1925

Kenneth was at the clan's new location when Creighton arrived. He was shocked at his condition. Ivan had managed the details of this transfer. He was now out seeking intelligence about why Creighton had been attacked. Luise arrived and immediately took up the role of nurse for her friend. She showed the strength of her character, as she tended to her beloved Creighton.

The following day Ivan came to Bromley and spoke with Kenneth. They agreed that Samuel should be warned about the actions of the French government. Kenneth had received a letter from Samuel. He had continued to bluster his feelings but had also asked more about the warnings Kenneth had included in his letter.

'This will give him something else to think about, apart from you and Creighton!' Ivan offered.

Kenneth asked, 'Do you think he was behind Creighton's beating?'

'We can't be entirely sure. Based on what I've learned, it's not likely. My sources believe the gang in question had run across some setbacks, including having some of their number arrested. I think they were searching for possible snitches. Somehow their attention centred on Creighton, and naturally, they stumbled across things that don't seem to add up. It was probably enough to mark him out. Assuming he recovers, he won't be much use around London for a number of decades!' Ivan suggested.

'Now, what about Dianna?' Ivan inquired.

Kenneth stood looking at Ivan before asking, 'Do you think it wise to take on a risky task, when our main operation may have been compromised?'

Ivan shook his head and said, 'If we wait, we will miss this year's opportunity to free Dianna. Hiding out here won't make the situation any safer. We might as well try to do something positive.'

'It may risk so many of us if it goes wrong,' said Kenneth, concerned.

'Perhaps it's time we took some chances.'

'Let's ask the others,' Kenneth concluded

Ivan nodded.

17 Bastille Day

1925

Dianna had advised the 'clan' that prior to every Bastille Day, she was taken to Paris and kept in an apartment. In the days before 14 July, the French authorities held internal meetings with the military, police and other key departments. Dianna observed these meetings to check the participants. She would look for any inappropriate individuals. Any participant who showed signs of having problems with the government would be identified to her keepers.

French Security did not know how Dianna accomplished these feats but knew she was accurate and reliable.

Each day once the meetings were over, Dianna was taken back to the secure apartment where she was held until after the Bastille Day celebrations were over. She spent Bastille Day in seclusion in the apartment. The door was guarded in the corridor, as was the stairwell, and front and rear entrances to the building. Bars on the windows were part of the apartment's furnishings.

Normally after breakfast, a supply of cold food was available in the apartment. Her captors never disturbed her again until the following morning (15 July), when they would escort her to the railway station.

Kenneth had contacted Jacques and got him to check with their mole who lived in the village close to the Countess' Chateaux. His response was that everything seemed normal there. Nothing appeared to be out of the ordinary. Their mole would advise Jacques should the Countess leave the area.

The clan decided they should proceed with an attempt to liberate Dianna.

*****

April 1925

George visited Paris to reconnoitre the area around the apartment, including the building itself. He developed the plan to free Dianna.

The apartment was in a five-story building on a street that radiated from the Place de Victor Hugo. A number of side streets and alleys branched out from this street. A police station was located about 200 metres from the building. Should things go wrong, the guards could rapidly call in reinforcements.

Like so many streets in Paris, there was a steady stream of pedestrians, horse-drawn traffic and motor vehicles on the street. In this busy environment, the activities of three people would not be easily noticed.

At each end of the street, there were a number of cafes and restaurants, which could help both as places for observing the scene and satisfy thirst or hunger.

George's plan called for three of the clan to be directly involved in its execution. One other member would also be in Paris. To try to blend into the Paris scenery, it was decided they would settle in a month before Bastille Day.

Frederick was chosen because Dianna had seen him in 1870. Luise and Elizabeth were needed because they both spoke superb French, and as women, they were less likely to attract suspicion. Kenneth was chosen to be the person in reserve. They would employ telephones during the extraction. He was the most competent at ensuring this would be done effectively.

Four chirpers would be required to act as decoys. They would know nothing about why they had been hired and would be treated to a vacation in central Paris, followed by three days' vacation in the French countryside.

Lastly, a team of two French burglars were required. Their reward would be money!

*****

Saturday
11th July 1925

Kenneth drank tea as he waited by the window of an apartment, six roads from where the Countess was kept. The telephone rang.

Frederick announced, 'Pleasant walk. Did not see Raymond.'

Kenneth replied with general conversation and hung up.

He knew Frederick had deliberately exposed himself to Dianna's view, as she was taken from the apartment to a waiting car. His cover was of a man enjoying a morning stroll. He had been enjoying a stroll like this for two weeks now. The code words 'pleasant walk' confirmed to Kenneth that Dianna had clearly seen him. His following phrase using the code word 'Raymond' told Kenneth that he felt he had not been followed. If he had used the code word 'Bernard,' then Kenneth would have known he suspected he had been noticed and possibly followed.

Kenneth waited, but no further phone calls were received.

*****

Luise had waited until the car containing Dianna had departed before she entered the street and followed in Frederick's footsteps. She did not detect any suspicious auras from people on the street, or from the plain-clothes police outside the apartment building. Should she have seen worrying auras, she would have found a telephone and called Kenneth. Having seen nothing to be concerned about, she had the day to herself.

Elizabeth had been observing the rear entrance to the apartment. She did not detect any unusual auras from the guards there or from the people she saw on the street.

This performance was repeated for the next two days. No unusual signs were seen in the auras of the people around Dianna, nor around people in the streets. It was evident Dianna was aware of Frederick and was hiding her recognition from her guards. They very careful that Dianna did not see Luise or Elizabeth.

Kenneth rented a taxi on the second evening and drove past the government building where the meetings were held. He studied the people as they came and went, but he detected no unusual auras. They all appeared to be going about their normal business activities, which was reassuring.

Bastille Day dawned and the team rose early. In mid-morning, Frederick with the two burglars, entered the apartment building adjacent to Dianna's, through the rear entrance. Luise kept watch to check if the guards next door had noticed anything unusual. No other unusual behaviour was seen from others around the building.

Once inside, Frederick and the burglars took the elevator to a floor, one level above Dianna's apartment. They checked that the corridors were not being monitored before approaching a specific door. Tools appeared. In a short time, the door opened and all three entered. While Frederick searched the apartment, the burglars waited by the entrance. The occupants had received an offer of a three-day visit to a Chateau, which had recently been converted to a hotel. They had enthusiastically accepted.

Frederick went to the front windows and arranged the curtains differently in each. Elizabeth was walking towards the building and noted the signal. He could see her signal telling him she had not seen any danger outside the building.

On the floor below this apartment were the private fitting rooms of a famous ladies outfitter. These were closed for the holiday.

Frederick nodded and the two burglars lifted the carpet and some floorboards. It was impressive how quietly they worked. He also noticed these men had already found some items of value and had placed them in a neat pile near the door.

Once a hole large enough for a person to go through had been made, they gently opened the ceiling below while holding the lathe and plaster. Some fell down, but mostly it was retrieved into the room above.

Frederick, and his helpers, quickly descended to the floor below, using a fine rope ladder, which had been wrapped around one of the burglars. Immediately, he took out a tape and measured three metres from the front wall. He then indicated the area he wanted opened, using chalk marks. It took over an hour for the two men to remove the plaster, and a section of brick before starting to remove the plaster on the wall beyond. All this had been accomplished, almost in silence.

Soon after they started to put holes in the plaster, they received assistance from Dianna; the wall was opened and Dianna crawled through. She had been prepared. Covering her clothes was a mutilated bed sheet, which she discarded along with the plaster crumbs it had accumulated. Her hair was tightly pushed under a man's hat, and she was wearing a man's suit with brown boots.

Without any fuss, the four climbed up into the apartment above. Frederick whispered to the two accomplices, 'Take what you want from the apartment. But do not get greedy, as you will be seen if you have a large load of booty. Take small things. Do not leave for another hour. Remember to be silent!'

Then he handed over a key and a letter. 'This is the bank where your payment is kept. Don't collect it for a couple of weeks, once the authorities have better things to do than chase after us!'

They could tell the burglars would obey the instructions and not double-cross them. Frederick was relieved. He had not relished the idea of pulling a gun on them to stop any unplanned activities. Dianna and Frederick left the apartment, went down the elevator, and walked out the front entrance. They turned left, away from the guards outside the building next door.

*****

Elizabeth had seen them leave. She waited ten minutes before walking to the apartment building next to Dianna's. Entering the front entrance, she went to the rear exit. Luise could see her from her vantage point and knew all was clear. Elizabeth retraced her steps and went to her hotel to ring Kenneth at 2:23 pm.

'I located Raymond at the Café Victor Hugo,' she confirmed. 'See you there.'

Elizabeth then left her hotel, and Luise signalled from across the street to indicate she had not been followed. Then they went their separate ways. One headed for Spain and the other for Switzerland.

Kenneth made phone calls to two couples they had sponsored to have a paid vacation across France. The couples had received new clothes and a money reward for doing this. They had been chosen because the women bore a resemblance to Dianna. Once he knew the couples were headed for railway stations, Kenneth vacated his room and caught a bus, which took him to the outskirts of Paris. There he picked up a motorcar and headed for the ferry at Calais.

The authorities would find out Dianna was missing by the next morning, at the latest. Should they check on her earlier, the hunt for her and any accomplices would be started in earnest. The hope was, the two sets of decoys would consume security resources so the clan members could make their escapes.

*****

Frederick drove Dianna to the outskirts of Paris. There were a number of small airfields around the city, which had been built during the war. He left the car at one of these and they approached an aeroplane. The pilot was Italian and would fly them to Germany. George had arranged for a change of clothes and a forged passport to be in the aircraft. At their destination, arrangements had been made for a friendly customs officer to be on duty.

Neither Frederick nor Dianna had been in an aeroplane before!

18 Dispersion

Friday
17th July 1925

When he returned from France, Kenneth found the new clan house in turmoil. George was keeping a low profile in the house due to one of his escapades going wrong.

They were sitting on the back veranda while a light drizzle blanketed the garden. At one time, the garden would have been kindly tended. Now it was overgrown. Kenneth felt he should take up gardening to try to improve it. For now, he sat gazing at the weeds, enjoying a Scotch with George.

George had developed a relationship with a married woman. She became a little too attached, and George ignored the danger signs.

George lamented, 'I really liked the lady!'

Unfortunately, the lady in question's husband is the jealous type and wealthy. Even more unfortunate is his brother is a senior officer in the London police service. The two siblings set about finding George to seek revenge. They were not particular about how they achieved this, which drove George to ground in Bromley.

This small satellite town to London is probably most famous for being the home of the young H.G. Wells. By the early 1920s, it was slowly being absorbed into the outer boroughs of London. With excellent rail connection to central London, it had attracted many commuters from the middle-class occupations carried out in the city. Good quality housing had swelled the leafy outskirts of the town. While further out, in places like Bickley, larger homes set in spacious gardens had been built. The town still had a vibrant market and main street, which not only served the town, but also the environs of North West Kent.

George did not like being cooped up. He complained to Kenneth, 'I can't stay here. In the past when these things have happened, I've always been able to move to another town. This time I worry these people have enough reach to have my description posted in every police station across the country.'

Kenneth realised George's life had been a series of adventures, punctuated by intense excitement as he slipped away from anguished husbands or fathers. Now the world was shrinking, and the enraged men had more opportunities to seek out George in other towns or even countries. *Not a life I would enjoy,* he thought. So he put his mind to how he might help George.

'Why not go somewhere in Europe, for a year or so?' Kenneth suggested.

'I'm not very invisible in Europe, and the ladies can be especially receptive.'

Kenneth thought for a few minutes. 'What does the clan have going on in Canada?'

George shrugged, 'Very little.'

Elizabeth had returned to Bromley the night before. She had reached Switzerland and then took a train across Germany to the Baltic. After an unpleasant ferry ride, she arrived in Sweden. A train took her to Oslo and another ferry to Hull. From Hull, it had been a few hours on a fast train to bring her to London.

She joined them on the veranda, poured herself a drink and offered, 'Luise will probably stay in Spain for a week or two. We should hear from her soon.'

Kenneth summarised George's dilemma. Elizabeth gave George a look somewhere between *what else can you expect* and *oh, dear*.

Ivan joined them and confirmed he had received word that Frederick and Dianna had arrived at the safe house in Gdansk.

George asked, 'What happens next?'

Kenneth replied, 'It's up to Dianna. She only knows about Frederick. It's essential she does not get to know of others until we know she can be trusted. He will not let her know anything of the clan. He'll also make sure she does not communicate with anyone until we can trust her. What she wants to do now is the real question.'

'She knows about Samuel.' Ivan offered. 'That should provide a topic of conversation, as a starting point for Frederick.'

Elizabeth mused, 'She has been held captive for a long time. I think she'll want to find her own way for a time, to re-establish her independence.'

They all considered the point.

'Still, it doesn't help us with George's problems,' she proposed.

'All I know is, having a miserable George around is tiring!' Ivan added.

'But where can I go?' George pleaded.

'Kenneth suggested Canada,' said Elizabeth. 'But it only has three big cities. Although it could work for perhaps a decade, it would be hard to blend into the background for decades. Perhaps if you developed our interests in Canada, New Zealand and Australia, it might provide a large enough population to blend into for fifty years or more. As we know, once you can be invisible for more than fifty years, it's possible to do it successfully for much longer.'

Ivan smiled, 'That's not a bad idea!'

George pointed out, 'Too big an area for an individual to properly manage. The travel times between places would be too long. I think it would need at least two people.'

Ivan thought for a few minutes. 'Ralph is ready to move on from his present activities. Perhaps he would like a brand new challenge?'

George immediately bucked up. 'We could work well together. Who better than a monk to keep an eye on a philandering bastard like me!'

Elizabeth broke into a belly laugh, 'Ralph made up for his celibate years within a year of being struck! Who would be keeping an eye on whom?'

Kenneth asked, 'A monk?'

George eyed Kenneth, 'It's a long story. You should get Ralph to tell you sometime. Elizabeth is right though. Ralph recognised the possibilities of his new capabilities almost immediately!'

The next day George discussed the idea with Ralph by telephone. He immediately liked it, and they started to plan how they could approach such a move.

It was nearly a week later that a dispatch arrived from Frederick. He reported that Dianna had been elated to be freed from the French authorities. She had been ready and competent as they made their escape. The first real problem arose when they reached the airfield. Once Dianna realised he expected her to board the aeroplane, she baulked. It took a lot of pleading with her to get her in the aeroplane. He pointed out that he would also be on board, and like her, he still saw such things as being almost magical. The pilot thought this was extremely funny! Finally, she climbed aboard. During the take-off, she clung to Frederick. She stopped doing that when he vomited!

He did not go into details about the landing but did say it was a good thing Dianna changed once they were on the ground. They passed through the border checks easily and were driven to a train station. After three changes of trains, they arrived in Gdansk.

Frederick explained to Dianna that he would offer to help her in any way he could. What he requested was a complete understanding of what the French knew of her, Lightning People, and general security issues. This was acceptable to her, but she insisted she would only stay for two days. Then she wished to be free.

He agreed and provided her with three forged passports, German, Swedish and Dutch. In order that she could establish a new life, he gave her money. Lastly, he told Dianna how to get in touch with him should the need arise. She should place advertisements in specific German and British newspapers, offering a fictitious property for sale. He specified the details of the address and house name she should use. By leaving a PO Box contact address with the newspapers, Frederick could then establish communication. No promises of assistance were given. At least she would not feel completely adrift on her own.

Dianna was as good as her word and was completely debriefed on all the matters he was interested in. Before she left, he warned her Samuel, the Lightning Person in America, was a rogue and could be very dangerous. She smiled and told him, she knew just how dangerous he could be. She had run across his activities before. In fact, she had been very surprised when she learned of the description given by the old French diplomat of the man on the ship. Dianna had thought Samuel might have been dead by now. It was one of the reasons she felt she should try to escape.

Then Dianna dropped a bombshell. The French authorities have learned the British are on the trail of at least one, if not two, Lightning People in England! They even believed one of them had only recently become a Lightning Person. Although, like the French, they do not actually know how this happens.

Dianna left Gdansk the next day. Frederick vacated the house the same day.

19 Attraction

Sunday
11th October 1925

Bruges was a relief from the recent chaos in London. Kenneth settled back into his apartment, overlooking the junction of two canals in Bruges. Being on the ground floor, he was only a few feet above the water and had a good view of the bridge, which crossed the main canal joining Langestraat to Hoogstraat. From there it was a few minutes' walk to the central square in Bruges. Many little restaurants and shops lined Hoogstraat, and so he could enjoy a meal without going far.

The medieval town had become popular after the Battle of Waterloo when pensioned-off British soldiers chose to stay in Belgium and made their homes in Bruges. This encouraged others to visit, and it enjoyed a period as a fashionable destination. The popularity waned as the century reached its end, and it was now a quiet, pleasant place to live.

Another advantage of having a good view of the bridge was he could see the people clearly while not being seen. If someone were to be watching the apartment, he would be able to see their aura. Should a person not have an aura, he could gain an advantage and discreetly study them.

Meanwhile, George had left for Canada while Ralph made plans to follow him. Frederick made a trip to Brussels to watch Jacques and Thomas for a week or so. By calling on their business as a delivery man, he was able to observe their auras and check if they seemed to be straying at all. By taking lodgings close by, he was able to see the comings and goings around the shop. In this way he satisfied himself they were not being watched and all seemed to be normal. Snoopers give clear signs of their activities in their auras, and so if enough time is spent observing a location, any such activities are easily noticed. Once this task was completed, he came to visit Kenneth in Bruges.

They enjoyed a pleasant meal at a canal-side bistro. The old town is surrounded by a medieval wall and is crisscrossed by canals. These canals link to the docks at the sea in Zeebrugge.

After reporting he believed Jacques and Thomas were still trustworthy, Frederick and Kenneth exchanged news. Frederick had also brought news of George and Ralph's plans. George had seen photographs of American gangsters in newspapers. In one George had been shocked to see Samuel at the back of a group. Clearly, Kenneth's warnings had either fallen on deaf ears, or Samuel had not been able to avoid the photograph. Ralph planned to leave for Canada in late summer of 1924.

In Sweden, Frederick had taken on the regions business activities from Ralph and Elizabeth. Introducing a new face there would help to quell any attention they may have stirred up.

Before he left, Frederick told Kenneth that Elizabeth had been busy looking at the British situation and how compromised they may be there. He wished Kenneth well as he left.

*****

The activities in the Netherlands, Belgium, France and Switzerland kept Kenneth busy for almost a year. He was especially careful when dealing with any French issues after the disturbance Dianna's liberation had caused. Frederick, in particular, kept well away from France!

*****

Sunday
8th November 1925

Elizabeth sent a dispatch out to the clan members. She had been at the Bromley house dealing with local matters, which included having the mail collected and read. To Kenneth, she wrote that she would visit him within the week and share the news with him directly.

After a meal, they exchanged news of the clan and local issues. Then Elizabeth shared an issue of particular interest to Kenneth.

'I wondered how the British authorities could have stumbled on the idea that there might be persons of interest in Britain,' she offered. 'What made them think one person was a recent development?'

'Perhaps Dianna was mistaken in her conclusions, or was lying to distract us?' Kenneth proposed.

'I thought of that and a number of other ideas. My thoughts went to Creighton and his recent run-in with his east end friends. That was too recent though!'

'Then I realised Frederick was known to Dianna and the French authorities for many years. When he escaped from France, he went to England. The French may have been able to pick up his trail and concluded he went there. No doubt they thought he was a German spy based in England. If I were the French, I would send some agents to Britain to look for him. If they did, it's likely they were detected or when the war broke out in 1914, the French shared knowledge with their ally, thinking he was a German—their common enemy.'

Kenneth thought for a moment before questioning, 'OK. That may explain one of the possible Lightning People, but what about the other?'

Elizabeth went on, 'I concluded it is you. How they found out about you, I could not immediately guess. I then remembered the French Extradition Warrant for Samuel. I'm sure the British found out about it and someone recognised Samuel's description from the 1918 incident when you were shot. Perhaps they looked into your background and noticed people who knew you and would refer to how you aged so well. When they went looking for you, they discovered you had disappeared.'

'Clearly, someone in the authorities has an unhealthy curiosity. Anyway, it's just guesswork,' he said.

'Actually, the man is called Inspector Trevor Brentworth!' Elizabeth boasted.

Kenneth stared at Elizabeth and whispered, 'What have you done?'

'It was easy, really,' she replied. 'I made a short vacation to your village in Wiltshire and just mooched about. Soon I noticed a local busybody called Mrs. Wilson, who was taking an interest in me. Her aura showed she had lots of curiosity and wanted very much to poke her nose in anywhere she can.'

Kenneth interrupted her, 'I remember her! She was nosey but seemed harmless.'

'I talked to her and she bragged she knew "everything that happens here." She also pushed me for my story so I played the secrecy card, which got Mrs. Wilson really interested. Luckily, as we chatted in the local shop, another older lady came in. Instantly, I saw Mrs. Wilson's aura change. The aura of the other lady also changed. Yet the two ladies ignored each other's presence. I knew I had Mrs. Wilson in my pocket! She and the other lady were clearly lovers. I had stumbled on a secret relationship, and I exploited it.'

'I told Mrs. Wilson, I represented a women's rights group and was following up on unscrupulous morality persecutions being undertaken by undercover police. They entered small communities with absurd avenues of investigation and found people who cooperated with them. Their real goal was to uncover the activities of men who have dubious morals, or women who do not live a 'normal' lifestyle. Mrs. Wilson went white when I told her this and started to fret about how she had to go home. I told her if she knew about such police activities, my group really needed to know all about it so we could prevent it elsewhere. We went to her house and she hurriedly told me all I needed to know. She expected her husband home shortly and so wanted me gone as soon as possible. I asked if she still kept in touch with Inspector Trevor Brentworth. She nodded. My advice to her was, never to show she knows of his real motives and to cooperate when asked to.

'Once I knew who to look for, it was fairly simple to track down our tormentor. Then I decided to discuss the situation with you.'

Kenneth looked at Elizabeth and thanked her for taking risks on his behalf.

"I did it for all of us. However, I would be lying if I didn't tell you I was concerned you may be in danger and I would not be happy if anything happened to you.'

Kenneth looked at Elizabeth as she stared at him. 'Are you saying you have feelings for me?'

'I have lived so long without love for a man and had almost given up on finding it. I am not like Luise, who can take what she needs from men around her. I have only done that when survival was the issue. Now I have met a man whom I could love, and remarkably, he is one of us. This is a big issue in my life, Kenneth. I might live for hundreds of years, and so might you. It brings a different perspective to *till death do us part*.'

Kenneth held out his hand and muttered, 'I never dreamed you might like me as well!'

Elizabeth walked over to him, leant down and kissed him. He pulled her down so that she sat astride his lap. Their kiss lasted a long time, then lapsed into panted breaths as they rejoiced together.

20 No Longer Alone

Saturday
16th January 1926

Elizabeth woke to the noise of a barge being coaxed under the bridge. Kenneth's bedroom window hung out over the canal, only 50 metres from the bridge. She then realised she could smell coffee!

'Have you been out?' she called.

'No. I have a hotplate and have made coffee. I thought its aroma might wake you.'

'Good. You are too set in your ways! Your regular walks are a bad idea. Also, this apartment is not suitable.' Elizabeth lectured.

'But, Elizabeth! I like the Hotel Langestraat. In particular, I like this apartment.'

'When we are together, please call me Ailsa. It is more familiar to me than Elizabeth. No one alive calls me Ailsa now, so I would like it if you did.'

She got up and went to the window seat. As she gazed out at the canal, Kenneth brought her coffee.

'No croissants, I'm afraid.'

Elizabeth looked along the canal at the bridge and the buildings beyond.

'This hotel's entrance is almost at the end of the bridge. It's really the only way in and out. You cannot see who may be watching the entrance or the bridge without going out into the street,' she told him. 'I suppose I'll have to move here and keep an eye out for you!'

'That would be very nice for me,' he smiled. 'But the clan has such a lot of things to be done. You can't be here all the time. Neither of us can. Besides, is it a good idea for both of us to be in one place?'

She had been thinking the same thing but had hatched a plan.

'We won't live here together. I'll find a suitable place where I can see what's going on around this hotel. We can talk by telephone and visit each other. We will both be very busy rearranging the clan's business in the next year or so. When we need to travel, we must try to do our travelling at the same time. Neither of us will then be left here alone.'

'Good. I want to spend as much time as possible with you!'

Before she could respond, he took her hand and led her back to the bed. One kiss and they both flopped down, entwining their arms and legs around each other.

Elizabeth thought, *I never want to spend another 250 years without love*'

*****

Saturday
17th July 1926

She gazed out of the upper window of the apartment above the warehouse. From here Elizabeth could easily see the complete bridge, some of the roads on either side, the front of the hotel and Kenneth's bedroom window. From the apartment's rear window, there is a view down the three alleys, which lead to the small courtyard behind this building. Should anyone follow Kenneth here, she would be able to see.

By placing objects in either this window or Kenneth's bedroom window, they could signal each other their intention to visit. It was a simple strategy but coupled with a telephone call or another signal, it was very effective.

The owners of the warehousing business were happy when she approached them as an investor. From their auras, it was clear they were open to capital investment. Setting the share of the company for the investment was almost too easy. They had talked amongst themselves in front of her and their colouring showed they were prepared to accept a sensible degree of ownership)and hence profits) for a monetary investment. One of her requirements had been to use the apartment. A lawyer settled the contract details, and Elizabeth sent the contract to London where Ivan and Luise signed as the investors.

The owners were pleased to vacate the apartment and move to a small house just outside the town walls. They had become bored with living above their business and craved the quiet of the fields in the evenings.

Elizabeth thought getting this location would give her some piece of mind. From here she can see Kenneth regularly, and keep an eye on his security situation. Frustrating as it is for her, she understands his lack of paranoia about all aspects of their security. He has only had a few years of experience being a Lightning Person, while she and the clan members have had hundreds of years of living in the shadows.

What the owners of this business were not aware of is its value to the clan. Large numbers of shipments and packages come through the warehouse daily. It will be simple to route clan communications and shipments through the business. She just has to review the transactions and intercept or redirect those that are pertinent to the clan's business.

One of Elizabeth's tasks was to keep in touch with the other clan members. This could be in person, by mail or telephone. In Britain, Creighton is still recovering in Gloucester, while Ivan and Luise are in the London area. Frederick is holed up in Sweden. Ralph and George are building new business interests in Canada, Australia and New Zealand.

*****

Tuesday
14th September 1926

She had seen Kenneth return to the hotel and had surveyed the area for people who showed suspicious auras. No indications of trouble and so she put a flower in her window. Kenneth responded by changing the curtain position in his bedroom window. A few minutes later she saw Kenneth come out of the hotels front entrance, turn right and cross the bridge. She could see no one following him or taking an unusual interest.

Moving to the back window, Elizabeth surveyed the alleys, which lead to the courtyard below. Kenneth walked into one of the alleyways and looked up. She could see he was not being followed and so she moved the curtains. A few moments later, she opened the backdoor and he entered.

'Good to be back again,' he stated, as he hugged her to himself.

'Good to see you again too,' she said.

'How was London, Ailsa?'

"Ivan and Luise send their regards, 'she responded as she let them into the apartment. 'And Creighton seems to be on the mend. He is comfortably recuperating in a house on the outskirts of Gloucester. My friends, Beth and Kate, are nursing him through the recovery period. They have no idea he is like me. I told them he had been attacked and robbed in London. He is well enough now to take an interest in the clan's activities. In fact, he has written a note warning us all about Samuel. He believes Samuel is by nature a cunning creature. So he doesn't accept he is still in the US.'

Kenneth protested, 'I got a letter from Samuel sent from California! He says he has been wounded and had to flee there from Chicago to hide.'

Elizabeth understood Kenneth's objection. But she has known Creighton for a long time and knew he has good instincts.

'Creighton pointed out it is not very difficult to arrange to have a letter mailed in California. It doesn't mean the letter was written there! He also still believes someone motivated his attackers. Samuel fits the bill, as far as Creighton is concerned. Should Creighton be correct, it might mean he is in Britain or Europe?'

'I suppose it's possible,' Kenneth admitted, although the look on his face did not convince Elizabeth he really believed it.

'Before we have dinner, can we discuss Jacques and Thomas?' she asked.

'Fine,' he replied.' It will keep me away from a hot stove for a while.'

'It's wonderful you like to cook,' she said. 'Too often it's assumed as I am a female, cooking comes easily to me. Unfortunately, that is just not true!'

'What about our two friends?' Kenneth asked.

'We need to move them onto bigger things.' She proposed. 'In Amsterdam, we have a business that needs new leadership. Their present operation could be easily taken over by new hands. Jacques knows something of our nature and so should be carefully nurtured, by you. Thomas has done well with his studies and would make a good manager for the business.'

'What is this business?' he asked.

'It's a trading company with an associated haulage and shipping arm. If Thomas manages the trading side, Jacques could manage the haulage and shipping. This would put Jacques in a perfect position to handle many of our special packages. Coupled with the operation here in Bruges and others we have, it gives us a wonderful alternative to the postal services for many of our needs.'

'OK. Sounds like a good idea. I'll meet with Jacques and we can get things moving.'

'Before I get hot and sweaty in the kitchen—' Kenneth started to say but was interrupted by Elizabeth pulling him to her and kissing him.

You would think, after hundreds of years of lovemaking, it might get boring, she thought, *but it's never the same twice. Now with*

Kenneth, it is so special and I know our love will survive for centuries.

After they had dinner, Elizabeth returned to what was happening in London.

'Ivan followed up, through an intermediary, on how the lads are doing. A couple of the lads were tracked down by the east end ruffians and closely questioned about Creighton. They seemed pleased Creighton had been disposed of by someone. This at least will put Creighton far from their minds and allow him to recover in peace.'

'Ivan and Luise are still in Bromley, although Ivan has a flat overlooking the Bromley house. They have cleverly rigged a telephone line between the two buildings. Meanwhile, Luise has an 'Aunt' who resides with her. She believes Luise has to 'come of age' before she can collect her fortune. Therefore she needs a person to 'front' for her in the interim. It seems Luise complains her sex life is severely restricted by this arrangement. She also visits Creighton regularly and takes a close interest in his nursing.

'Frederick is taking no chances in Sweden. He will not travel to Germany or France until he is sure things have settled down. Unfortunately, they don't seem to be doing that. Inspector Brentworth has travelled to France. No doubt to meet with Leboudec, in order to coordinate their efforts to find you. Frederick is only too aware the French know about him, and he is now particularly keen to keep to himself!'

Kenneth interrupted her, 'Ailsa, you are a marvel. For the wife of a small holding farmer in rural Denmark, you have blossomed into an international agent of intrigue. I give thanks you are still the beautiful woman who left Denmark all those years ago, even if your mind has developed beyond recognition in that time.'

Elizabeth hugged him and let her thoughts dwell on what he had said. To show her appreciation, she gently kissed his forehead as it lay cradled in her arms.

'I'm not sure that is entirely correct. I have learned lots of things in those years, languages, finance, how to recognise a danger, cunning ways to avoid being noticed, and many more besides. I do not think I have actually changed. Inside, I still have my faith, although it rarely shows. I believe I still think in the same manner and have the same intelligence. What is different is my level of training and stored experiences. So, don't fret Kenneth., I am really just an innocent farmer's wife who has fallen for a handsome foreigner.'

Kenneth rolled over and gently grabbed her. ''This foreigner sees a woman who has been deprived for far too long, and he intends to redress the situation.'

Elizabeth giggled, as Kenneth fumbled with her blouse buttons before she pulled his head back and kissed him.

21 Reunion

Tuesday
18th January 1927

Samuel leaned on the bar and smiled at the lady next to him.

'You seem too nice a person to be following your profession,' he queried.

She smiled and replied, 'Even nice people have to eat. What you pay me to spy for you, doesn't pay the bills.'

"Your letter indicated you believe you may have found who I am looking for?' he asked.

'Perhaps I have. Is there a bonus if I have?' she replied.

'If you have, I shall reward you well. If not, I'll be displeased. I don't like to waste my time!' Although he could see from her aura, she was sincere and confident.

'Follow me,' she instructed.

He followed the young woman out the bar and down an alleyway. This town looked much as it did in the early 1800's when it was a popular resort and retirement local. There were many small hotels and private houses, huddled around the network of canals, which dissect the town. *It has hardly changed at all*, he thought.

She followed the canal path towards the centre of town and then turned into a doorway. This was the back door to a restaurant located next to a bridge which crosses one of the main canals.

Even at this late hour, barges were being sailed or pulled along the canals. Many workers took a break in the restaurant. There was a small crowd gathered there, as they traversed the tables and entered a stairwell.

She spoke over her shoulder, 'They won't pay any attention to you. You'll be seen as one of my clients.'

At the top of house, she entered a small attic and pointed to the window.

'He likes to take an early morning walk. You'll get a good view of him as he comes out of the hotel opposite. Apparently, he has been living there for a year or more.'

Samuel studied the window and asked, 'Do we need to open the window to see him clearly?'

'No. It's a fine view, whether it's open or closed,' she responded.

'What time will he take his walk?' he asked.

'About 7:00,' she answered.

'What are you doing up at seven in the morning?' he wondered.

'Shooing out clients and keeping an eye on your friend,' was her reply.

'How did you find him?' Samuel asked, suspicious, as her aura was showing a higher level of self-confidence than he expected.

'Your description was very good. The fact he is English helped a lot. I spoke with a few people I know, saying I was trying to trace a special client. One of them remembered an Englishman he had recently seen in this area. So I rented this room, thinking I might watch who crossed the bridge. One day I was taking a fella up here and heard a man speaking to the waitress in the restaurant. I took a quick look and realised it was who you wanted to find. I went to follow him, and to my surprise, he walked straight across the road and into the hotel. The rest was easy!'

Samuel had watched her aura as she had recounted her tale. It showed honesty and pride. He was satisfied.

Samuel smiled and muttered, 'So naïve.'

The girl sternly looked at Samuel and said, 'I'm not naïve! I know how to look after myself.'

'Not you, young lady,' he said.

She was clearly puzzled, why he called her a young lady. He couldn't be more than three years older than her.

Samuel looked around the small room and said, 'So we have to wait until the morning. Perhaps you should show me just how you earn your living while we wait?'

She smiled, but said, 'That's extra!'

'Oh, yes' he replied.

*****

He sat at the closed window from 6:00 am until his quarry strode out of the hotel opposite, just over an hour later. He knew the man immediately even though he could not check his lack of an aura through the glass of the window.

He watched as he walked across the bridge towards the centre of town.

'Where does he go on these morning walks?' he asked the girl.

She was busy dressing and curtly replied, 'I don't know! He is usually back by about 9:30.'

Samuel spun around, left the window and grabbed her arm.

'You shall keep this room as your business place for the rest of the year. Do not change your habits, no matter what happens. Do you understand me?' he demanded.

She nodded.

'Above all! You have never seen me!' he instructed.

Again, she nodded, now with fear in her eyes. Samuel turned towards the door and spoke with his back to her.

'A sizeable sum will be sent to the postal address you are using. There will be a good bonus and a special amount for you being so good at your job! Do not spend freely as it will attract attention. Use the money wisely.'

With these words, he left her, crossed the restaurant and exited by the backdoor.

*****

That evening Samuel waited by one of the gates to the walled city of Bruges. A car pulled up and he got into the passenger seat.

'We will drive through the town a couple of times to make sure you know the route to take out of town,' Samuel told the driver.

He gave instructions as to which road to follow and they drove down a narrow, shop-lined street to the bridge over the canal. They did not stop. Over the bridge, the road went straight into the main square in the centre of the town. It is ringed with medieval buildings with ornate stonework and arched entrances. They drove directly across the square, exiting on a narrow road which curved left, before going almost straight to another gate in the city wall. Once outside the wall, the buildings ceased and the road ran through well-tended fields.

The car stopped next to another car sitting at the roadside. He looked at the other car.

'It seems to be a faster car than this one.'

The driver said, 'It is!'

'Is it ready to go?' he asked.

'Warmed up and ready.'

This journey was repeated twice more. Then on the third practice, they stopped briefly outside the hotel, before proceeding.

When back at the city gate, Samuel informed the driver, 'This time you stop outside the hotel and keep the engine running. I should be back quickly.'

By now it was dark with a slight drizzle in the air. There were few people on the streets as the car pulled up outside the hotel.

Samuel got out of the car and entered the small lobby. A skinny man was in attendance at the front desk. Samuel walked up to him, placed a 20-franc note on the desk and asked in perfect French, 'What room is the English gentleman staying in?'

The man was so surprised by this request and the money proffered, he mumbled number four and pointed towards a small inner courtyard at the rear of the lobby, visible through French doors. Samuel immediately strode towards the French doors, while the man started to protest. Samuel continued across the small courtyard, down two steps and turned left to a door with a large brass number four.

He tapped on the door and in an excellent imitation of the skinny mans, tone and accent, he said, 'Pardon Monsieur'.

He heard movement and the sound of the door being unlocked when there was a loud shout from behind him. Instantly Samuel threw his weight onto the door before it could be re-bolted. He almost fell into the room. As he regained his balance he pulled a revolver from inside his jacket. His quarry had retreated across the chamber and was about to clamber up four steps to a door into an adjacent room. He immediately knew there had been no mistake. His prey had no aura!

Samuel raised the revolver and fired two shots at Kenneth, as he plunged through the doorway into the adjacent bedroom. He could see he had missed him with both shots. The door and wall bore the scars of the errant bullets.

Five strides took Samuel to the steps and the bedroom door. As he vaulted up the steps, he saw Kenneth had opened the window and was starting to climb through. He was on Samuel's right side so he had to get into the room, spin right, before he could aim and fire. As he fired Kenneth tumbled out of the open window. Samuel saw blood splatter against the glass, as Kenneth dropped from his view. He ran to the window and leaned out, only to see the grey water of the canal. Blood was floating to the surface just below. He emptied the last three bullets into the water, then turned and raced towards the door.

He ran out the apartment. Across the small courtyard and reached the lobby. The man there had the telephone to his ear. His eyes opened wide when Samuel appeared.

Samuel dug his hand into his jacket pocket and pulled out a small automatic pistol. He raised the pistol as the man yelled, 'I won't tell!'

He fired four shots into the man's chest before the man collapsed onto the floor.

Samuel spun around, strode through the door and got into the car.

"Drive!' he yelled.

'Close that window!' He added.

The response was a slight shake of the head and, 'The windows are misting up. I need to see to drive!'

The car sped through the town and out the other gate. Three kilometres out of town it pulled up next to the larger vehicle. They both quickly got out of the car and into the parked car. The car's engine fired, it jumped, as first gear was engaged and it pulled rapidly away into the night.

They drove in silence for more than an hour. Then Samuel broke the silence.

'You've really taken to driving.'

'When you have been cooped up in a prison, even a luxurious one, you crave being free. Driving is providing me with a wonderful sense of freedom, I've never experienced before.' Dianna explained.

Samuel stared at Dianna. It was over two hundred years ago since she had been spirited away from him. She had diverted their pursuers away from him, so he could escape. They had been sharing their lives for over 500 years before that rupture. No matter how he tried, he had not been able to locate her, until 1918, when he saw her at one of the meetings in Paris.

Samuel had arranged things exactly so he could free her when the Englishman had appeared. Having Kenneth in the same building where her rescue was to occur, could have been disastrous for them both. Rage overcame him, and he shot Kenneth. Then he had to run, to avoid joining Dianna, as a captive, or worse.

Now he had his revenge!

Dianna laughed.

Samuel stared at her.

'What fools! I couldn't believe they actually freed me and then let me go my own way. It took me a week or two to realise, they were not following me. They had actually let me go free! Then I understood. They are not aware we are together!' Dianna mused.

Samuel growled, 'At least we have rid ourselves of two of them.'

'Are you sure Creighton is dead?' she asked.

'I grilled the people in London very thoroughly and their aura's clearly showed they sincerely believe he is dead. That leaves the one called Frederick!' he stated.

'You are assuming there are just three of them.' She cautioned.

Samuel thought about this for a minute or two. Then said, 'You might be right!'

Her response was exactly as he expected, 'From now on, Samuel, I will decide on how we deal with the world around us. You run our schemes and I'll think them through. We must avoid this propensity to violence, you have recently discovered. Like before, let others get their hands dirty, while we reap the benefits. Do you agree?'

Samuel smiled, 'Most certainly! Dianna, we are a wonderful team. With your skill at thinking things through and my cunning, there is no stopping us. But there is one thing, I have to admit, Kenneth got right. The world is changing and it is getting more difficult to easily change identities.'

She smiled at him and said, 'Good.'

A border crossing came into view. When stopped, she provided the guard with German passports and answered his questions in perfect German.

Then the guard asked, 'Where are you going at such a late hour? Home?'

Dianna replied, 'We have received an invitation from an important person and do not want to be late.'

The guard asked, 'Who is this important person?'

Samuel replied, 'My friend, Adolf Hitler.'

Immediately, the guard stood straighter.

'I know of this man. I think he will one day be a great man, for Germany. Please go on your way!'

As they drove away Dianna commented, 'You do make useful friends, my dear.'

Samuel responded, 'He is very useful, and will prove to be even more so in future. But he is extremely dangerous. We must not underestimate his deceit and cunning.'

They both looked at each other and coldly smiled, at their joint hidden powers.

*****

Dedication

To Rhiain and my parents, Winn and Dick.
Without your belief in me, nothing would have happened.

Acknowledgements

I owe a debt of gratitude to all the teachers who persevered in teaching me to read. Once I mastered the skill, it has been a treasured gift.

My tutor at university told me I should write stories. At the time I thought he was pulling my leg. Thank you, Bill Crease, for putting the idea of writing stories into my head.

I owe Edda Buck a big thank you for patiently listening to the idea behind this story when it first occurred to me.

Thank you Richard, Kevin, Lisa and Emily for your advice and support.

Joining the NOTL Writers' Circle galvanised my resolve to push forward with my tale. They also showed me it is possible to publish a book. Thanks to all at NOTL Writers' Circle: http://www.notlwriterscircle.com/

Thank you, Sally Basmajian, for your advice on Chapter 1, and for your encouragement to publish my work.

Deborah Glover encouraged me to push on with this particular story. She allowed me to read her each chapter as it arrived at the pencil and paper stage. Her delight in hearing each chapter helped me reach for the next. Special thanks for your encouragement.

Thank you, Nancy Kay Clark, Editor of *Commuter Lit*. Nancy provided me with an in-depth critic of the first five chapters—extremely helpful. Even if I did not follow all the advice offered, I believe the end result did profit from the critic Nancy provided. http://commuterlit.com/

I am especially grateful to, Judy McHattie, Murray Wilcox and Richard J Wright for reading the manuscript and offering their thoughts. I tried to respect their ideas as I made the final edits.

I owe thanks to my painting friends for being so supportive and asking me to read chapters to them. Their positive responses helped me along the way. So thanks to Albert, Marilyn, Deborah, Lynnette, Murray, Judy, and Suzanne.

Lastly, I am very lucky to have had the support of Shawna Lessard with Editorial Advice and Copy Editing. Thank You.

Lightning People: Discovered

In 1903 Kenneth’s life was transformed.
He could see our Auras.
We can’t see anything different about him.
But even he did not realise the full extent of the changes he had endured.
Then he discovered the Lightning People. Although not immortal, they have lifespans vastly greater than ours.
But amongst the Lightning People are Rogues who are selfish, cunning and dangerous.

About the Author

Richard P. West is a retired engineer who lives in Canada. Richard's career has taken him to all continents (except Antarctica) and has included a wide range of experiences.

He has always loved to read about new things, discover people's life stories and enjoy fiction. Exposed to Welsh poetry and verse by his wife, he has a soft spot for Dylan Thomas. But whether it is Dickens, Lawrence or Czerneda, it's the story they tell that fascinates.

Later in life, Richard realised that although he loved to read what people have written, he had little idea how they did it. Never one to just shrug off a question, he set out to learn how to write. The journey of learning something of this craft has been and is most rewarding. Richard has written a number short stories and is working on another novel.

Richard recently discovered the NOTL Writers Circle and is now an active member.

www.richardpwest.ca

Lightning People – Summary Table

	Name	Date Struck	Age
1	Kenneth (Clan)	1903	40
2	Creighton (Clan)	1472	30
3	Elizabeth (Clan)	1655	35
4	Luise (Clan)	1742	17
5	Ivan (Clan)	390	44
6	George (Clan)	1828	51
7	Frederick (Clan)	1144	24
8	Ralph (Clan)	1360	31
9	Tara (Loner)	590 BC	25
10	Dianna (Turned)	unknown	40
11	Samuel (Rogue)	before 1000 BC	25

Manufactured by Amazon.ca
Bolton, ON

38571310R00092